MARY ANNE TO THE RESCUE

Other books by
Ann M. Martin

Leo the Magnificat
Rachel Parker, Kindergarten Show-off
Eleven Kids, One Summer
Ma and Pa Dracula
Yours Turly, Shirley
Ten Kids, No Pets
Slam Book
Just a Summer Romance
Missing Since Monday
With You and Without You
Me and Katie (the Pest)
Stage Fright
Inside Out
Bummer Summer

THE KIDS IN MS. COLMAN'S CLASS series
BABY-SITTERS LITTLE SISTER series
THE BABY-SITTERS CLUB mysteries
THE BABY-SITTERS CLUB series

MARY ANNE TO THE RESCUE

Ann M. Martin

AN
APPLE
PAPERBACK

SCHOLASTIC INC.
New York Toronto London Auckland Sydney

The author gratefully acknowledges
Peter Lerangis
for his help in
preparing this manuscript.

Cover art by Hodges Soileau

ISBN 0-590-69215-1

12 11 10 9 8 7 6 5 4 3 2 1 7 8 9/9 0 1 2/0

Printed in the U.S.A. 40

First Scholastic printing, June 1997

"There it is!" Abby Stevenson jumped up from her seat in the airport waiting room. She began waving at an incoming airplane. "Hi, Dawn! Hi, Jeff!"

Kristy Thomas squinted out the window. "Air New Zealand?"

"Oops," Abby replied. "Wrong plane."

"Maybe Dawn and Jeff took the scenic route," Claudia Kishi suggested.

Stacey McGill gave her a Look. "From Los Angeles?"

"They're now nine minutes late," Mallory Pike complained.

"Patience, patience," said my stepmother, Sharon.

My dad looked up from his newspaper. "We could play twenty questions or something."

"Can I start?" Jessi Ramsey piped up. "Let's see, I'm thinking of a — "

"Attention, please!" blared a voice over the

airport loudspeaker. "Flight three-oh-four from Los Angeles, due in at two-fifteen, will be arriving approximately one hour late."

"One hour?" groaned Kristy, sinking back into her seat. "What do we do now?"

Abby shrugged. "We could lengthen our game. Make it two hundred questions."

"I saw a really cool shop on the way in," Stacey suggested.

"What about the video arcade?" asked Claudia.

"Or the cafeteria," I chimed in.

"Now *there's* an idea," Dad said. "Would you girls like a snack? Our treat."

Zoom. Forget about the clothes and the videos. Off we went.

Thank goodness. I was starving. All day long I'd been so nervous I could barely eat.

You see, Dawn and Jeff Schafer happen to be my stepsiblings. She's thirteen, like me, and he's ten. Dawn is the only sister I have ever had, and I miss her *sooooo* much. I count the days between her visits.

Dawn and Jeff live in Palo City, California, with their dad. I live in Stoneybrook, Connecticut.

Why do two stepsisters live so far apart? Well, it's a long story. A tale of two coasts.

It starts in Palo City, where Dawn was born and raised. When Sharon and Mr. Schafer divorced, Sharon decided to move back to her hometown, which happened to be Stoneybrook. Jeff couldn't make the adjustment. (Eventually he begged to move back with his dad, and Sharon let him.) Dawn liked Stoneybrook, though. She and I became friends, and we soon discovered an incredible Big Secret — my dad and her mom had been madly in love in high school. Well, we went right to work. We reintroduced them, wedding bells were soon chiming, and the rest is history.

Dad and I moved to Dawn's house, a two-hundred-year-old farmhouse. Dawn and I grew as close as if we'd known each other forever. Unfortunately, though, Dawn became homesick for California. Like Jeff, she felt she had to move back.

Which is why she's there and I'm here.

Sigh.

I, by the way, am Mary Anne Spier. My friends and I were waiting at the airport. Stoneybrook is a little more than an hour away, and I had managed to convince Sharon and my dad to take both cars to the airport, because the entire Baby-sitters Club wanted to surprise Dawn. (The BSC is a group I belong to, and I'll tell you all about it later.)

It wasn't easy to persuade my dad. He said that taking both cars was "overkill" and "a waste of gas."

He is Mr. Practical.

Sharon's response? "Come on, Richard, the more the merrier!"

Thank goodness Sharon hasn't grown homesick for California. She's so much fun. In many ways she's the opposite of Dad — she's relaxed and absentminded, and he's conservative and super-organized — but in a funny way they're a perfect match. Sharon has totally changed his life. Mine, too.

I didn't know what it meant to have a mom until I was thirteen. My real mother died when I was a baby. Dad raised me by himself.

I didn't mind being an only child. Dad took great care of me, even though he was strict. Kristy, my best friend, used to call him the King of Rules. It's kind of true. Until seventh grade I wasn't allowed to have my ears pierced. I had to keep my hair in pigtails and wear these long, little-girlish skirts all the time. Kids teased me about it. It took Dad forever to accept that I was growing up. Fortunately, he's changed a lot. If you saw me now you'd have no trouble believing I'm a thirteen-year-old eighth-grader. I have brown hair, which I wear short, and if you had to name my clothing style, you might call it preppy casual. And yes, I do have pierced ears.

Walking to the airport cafeteria, Dad and Sharon were like two lovebirds. Arm in arm, smiling away. Sharon looked so happy. She becomes very emotional whenever Dawn visits. (I think Dad does, too, but he doesn't show it.)

My friends and I slapped trays onto the metal rack and pushed them along. The foods of choice seemed to be salad and chips, except for Claudia the Junk Food Maniac, who selected chocolate pudding, a brownie with a scoop of chocolate ice cream, and a Ring-Ding.

As we took seats, Abby was cracking up at Claudia's tray. "You sure you don't want some sprouts with that?"

"For your information, chocolate is a high-energy foodstuff," Claudia informed her.

"Foodstuff?" Kristy murmured.

"Why do you need high energy to wait in an airport?" Stacey asked.

"The anxiety," Claudia said, unwrapping her Ring-Ding, "is exhausting."

We all dug in, giggling and chatting. Around us, the cafeteria was beginning to fill up. I noticed a family of five — a dad and a mom with two young boys and a girl — sitting a few tables away from us.

Kristy had her eyes on them. She's the founder and president of the BSC, and whenever she sees a family like that, you can almost see a neon light blinking in her head: CLIENTS . . . CLIENTS . . . CLIENTS . . .

"I wonder if they live in Stoneybrook," she said softly.

Stacey rolled her eyes. "Kristy, puh-leeze."

"Well, they *could,*" Kristy insisted. "Or they could know someone who does. The worst they could say is no."

Claudia's jaw dropped. "You're not actually thinking of asking them?"

"Well . . ."

"You would embarrass your best friends in the middle of a huge international airport?" Claudia barreled on. "You would bother this innocent family while they're trying to enjoy a peaceful meal?"

I glanced at the innocent family. The two older kids, who looked to be about six, were flinging french fries at each other. The youngest one, maybe three years old, was pushing her glass of milk over the edge of the table. The mom and dad were trying to eat between scoldings and disaster prevention.

Kristy was glancing at them warily. "Uh, maybe it wouldn't be such a great idea."

I caught a glimpse of the mom running off to the bathroom with the little one, who was covered with milk.

BANG! BANG! BANG!

The table-smacking was like sudden gunshots. I am a very patient, understanding, tolerant person, but this was too much.

We all turned to look.

The dad was standing up, his fists pounding the table.

I could not believe how rude he was being.

His chair skidded back, then fell over. He was leaning forward, legs spread apart.

His kids stopped flinging. They looked at him with big smiles, as if he were doing some silly impersonation.

Then the smiles disappeared.

"Oh my lord . . ." Stacey murmured.

The man's face was turning red. Around him, people were staring. He stopped banging and started flailing his arms jerkily. His mouth was open but he was making no sound.

"It's a heart attack!" someone yelled.

"Call a doctor!" another voice rang out.

Sharon was out of her chair like a shot. *"He's pointing to his throat!"* she blurted out.

She raced across the room, practically colliding with a busboy.

The man sank to his knees. His kids were frozen, in total shock.

I am watching someone die.

The words sneaked into my brain. I felt helpless. Dizzy. My throat was like sandpaper. My vision blurred. I could feel the blood rushing from my head.

Everything seemed to be happening underwater, slow and dreamlike. Sharon was behind the man now. He had slumped to the floor, propping himself up on one elbow. His face was practically purple.

She knelt down and wrapped her arms around his midsection. He must have weighed two hundred pounds, but she managed to lift his torso upright.

She dug her fists into the area below his ribcage. Then she pulled inward sharply.

Nothing happened.

She tried it a second time, and a third. The man was limp now. The kids were crying hysterically.

The fourth time, Sharon pulled so hard, I thought she'd break his ribs.

A chunk of something shot out of the man's mouth. He let out a loud, strangled-sounding shout.

Then I lost sight of them as a crowd began to close around the scene.

Slowly my own senses were coming back to me. My dad was in the crowd now. So were Kristy, Abby, Jessi, and Stacey. The man's wife was pushing frantically through the crowd, holding the little girl. Restaurant workers followed, with wet towels and small bottles — of what? Smelling salts? Medicine? Spring water? I had no idea.

"Mary Anne, are you all right?"

Mallory's voice startled me. I turned to see her looking up at me with concern.

"I'm fine," I replied.

"I think Sharon just saved that guy's life," Mal said.

"I hope so," was all I managed to reply.

Mal and I made our way across the floor. Most of the tables were empty now. The crowd around Sharon had swelled. Everyone was yakking away, asking questions. I could see a few people nodding and smiling.

Then someone started to applaud, and all the buzzing stopped. More people joined the clapping.

By this time Mal and I had worked our way to the front, near Kristy and our other friends.

The man was sitting on the chair with a weary smile, breathing hard. His wife was wiping his forehead with a white towel, which she also used to wipe tears from her eyes. His kids were in his lap, hugging him tightly.

Sharon and Dad were standing nearby, their arms around each other's shoulders. Sharon looked a little bewildered at the loud cheering. She was nodding and muttering, "Thank you."

"Unbelievable," Kristy said admiringly. "I've never seen anyone move so fast."

I ran to Sharon. She looked up at me with a big smile. "He's okay."

"That was such quick thinking," I said.

Sharon shrugged. "I didn't even think, really. I just did it. My instincts took over."

"Well, I certainly couldn't have done it," Dad said.

"There's nothing to it," Sharon replied. "Really. Just your basic Heimlich maneuver. It's the first thing you learn in any first-aid course."

Now a group of white-uniformed medics was being led through the crowd by an airport official.

As the official began asking Sharon questions, I hung back in the crowd. Kristy, Claudia, Abby, Jessi, Stacey, and Mallory were talking excitedly. Total strangers were joining in the conversation. Everyone was praising Sharon.

But I didn't have either of those feelings. I was still feeling stunned.

And ashamed.

I hadn't done a thing when the emergency started. I had just frozen up.

Tears began rolling down my cheeks.

"It's okay, Mary Anne," Jessi said softly. "He's all right."

"I — I just stood there," I mumbled. "Like a statue."

Abby nodded sympathetically. "So did the rest of us. Good thing Sharon was here, huh?"

"Yeah," I said. "A great thing."

I didn't want to mention what was really on my mind.

What if Sharon hadn't been there?

The man might not have survived. Everyone in his family, all his kids, would have been devastated.

And I couldn't have done anything.

The crowd was beginning to thin out now. The airport official was offering the family a free meal. The man and woman were nodding politely, but I could tell they weren't really paying attention. They were clinging together, so happy and grateful.

Their lives were going to go on. All because of my stepmother.

In the background, I heard an announcement about Dawn's flight, but I didn't catch the details.

My mind was racing. I wanted to say something to the man, but I couldn't bring myself to. What would I say? "I'm the daughter of the woman who saved you. You know, the girl who almost fainted?"

I felt like such a chicken.

"Ta-da!" Claudia sang. She emerged from her bedroom closet, holding a lumpy brown object wrapped in plastic, and a container of green mush.

"Mmm, boulders and boogers," said Abby. "What a nice way to greet Dawn."

"Gross, Abby!" Stacey exclaimed.

Jessi and Mallory were hysterical. Doubled over with laughter.

Claudia held up the two things and read from their labels: " 'Yeastless seven-grain molasses bread' and 'organic mint tabouli.' " She grinned. "Dawn food."

Dawn was sitting in the middle of Claudia's bed, squidged between Stacey and Abby. "Yum, thanks!" she said, taking the food. "You guys don't know what you're missing."

That's Dawn. She is the world's number-one health-food freak. She calls hamburgers "processed cow corpses." When we became stepsisters, she and Sharon forced my poor dad to return almost an entire load of groceries he'd bought because the produce was "tainted with chemical insect killer."

Dawn's also passionate about the environment — recycling, global warming, alternative packaging, you name it. Some kids at school used to make fun of her, but she didn't care a bit. She's a real individual.

It was so great to have her back home. And just in time for our Friday Baby-sitters Club meeting.

Dawn is the BSC's honorary member. She always comes to meetings when she visits. And Claudia always remembers to provide some "Dawn food."

"And now, for the rest of us!" Claudia announced, pulling a box of Yodels and a bag of potato chips from under her bed.

Claudia tossed them around the room, and we all dug in. (No, Dawn has not totally converted me to health foods, although she's still trying.)

Luckily for Dawn, she's found a group of friends in California who share her beliefs. They formed a baby-sitting organization called the We ♥ Kids Club.

Well, that's what most of us call them. Kristy usually puts a "so-called" before the word *club.* (On her nice days. I have heard her refer to them as the We R Lazy Club, too.) They're very informal about meeting times and rules. Kristy believes a real club has to have officers and dues and strict procedures.

Like the club *she* formed — us!

The idea came to her one day as she watched her mom desperately calling all over town to find a sitter for Kristy's younger brother, David Michael. Kristy couldn't believe how inefficient that was. What Stoneybrook needed was a central phone number for baby-sitters.

She knew Claudia had her own private phone. And back then, the three of us lived on the same block. Stacey lived nearby, too. So we became the first Baby-sitters Club members.

We meet in Claudia's room three times a week, Mondays, Wednesdays, and Fridays, from five-thirty to six. During that half hour, Stoneybrook parents call to set up baby-sitting jobs.

As secretary, my job begins when a call comes in. First we take down the information and promise to call back. Then I check the BSC record book, which contains our official calendar. On the calendar, I keep track of every BSC member's conflicts — lessons, doctor appointments, family trips, and so on. I announce who's available, and we all decide who'll take the job. Then we call back the client to finalize.

At the back of the record book, I keep up an

alphabetical client list with phone numbers, addresses, rates, and any important information about our charges. Because we can't guarantee the same family the same sitter each time, it's crucial to record new developments in our charges' lives, for instance, allergies, fears, habits, problems. (We also maintain a club journal, called the BSC notebook. Kristy makes us write about each of our jobs in it.)

Am I making Kristy sound unbearable? She's not. She's kind and funny and loyal. Her mind just goes about two speeds faster than everyone else's. That makes her a little impatient and bossy.

Kristy also loves to be in control, which is why she's a perfect BSC president. She runs us like a company. But don't think we sit around with three-piece suits and laptops. We don't. Our meetings are fun, and, as you've probably figured out, we're all great friends.

Personally, I think Kristy's title should be Creative Director. Ideas are her great passion. She practically breathes them out. For one thing, she loves figuring out ways to advertise the club. If a local fair is announced, you can be sure we'll set up a baby-sitting booth. Kristy's best ideas, though, are kid-oriented. Like Kid-Kits, which are boxes of old toys, games, books, and kid-friendly odds and ends we take to our jobs. Kristy's constantly planning talent shows and sports events for kids. She even organized a softball team, called Kristy's Krushers, for our charges who aren't in Little League.

Kristy and I look alike. Sort of. We both have brown hair and brown eyes, and we're both just a little over five feet tall. Personalitywise, we're not alike at all. I could never be as forceful as Kristy. Or as opinionated. I'm shy, I hate confrontation, and I tend to cry a lot. (My boyfriend, Logan Bruno, keeps extra tissues in his pocket whenever we go to a sad movie.)

Some people are surprised that Kristy and I are best friends. But it doesn't surprise me at all. We've known each other since we were babies. Kristy used to live next door to me on Bradford Court with her mom, dad, and brothers. But shortly after David Michael was born, Mr. Thomas abandoned the family. Just walked away without warning. (Needless to say, Kristy does not like talking about him.) Things were tough for a long time. Kristy and her older brothers worked hard to make up for Mr. Thomas's absence. Then one day Kristy's mom met and married a Prince Charming who whisked her off her feet and took her away to a castle on a hill. Well, actually, the prince was a middle-aged businessman named Watson Brewer who happened to be a millionaire. The castle was a mansion in Stoneybrook's wealthy neighborhood.

Kristy's family has doubled in size, from five to ten. First of all, Watson's two children from a previous marriage, Karen and Andrew, live at the mansion every other month. Second, Kristy's mom and Watson adopted a two-and-a-half-year-old girl named Emily Michelle, who was born in Vietnam. Then, to help take care of Emily, Kristy's grandmother moved in with the Thomas/Brewers. Actually, if you count the pets in the house at any given time (a puppy, a cat, a hermit crab, two goldfish, and a rat) I guess you could say the family has more than tripled.

Not every BSC member has had family-morphs like Kristy's and mine. Claudia, for example, has had the same family since birth — her mom, her dad, and her sister, Janine. Janine is an honest-to-goodness certified genius. She's in high school but takes college courses. Mr. and Mrs. Kishi are like grown-up versions of her. They're very proper and hardworking. When the Kishi girls were younger, their parents used to put colored stars on a chart for every test score over 90 — pink stars for Claudia, yellow for Janine. They stopped when the yellow ran out and the pink box hadn't been opened.

Claudia has always felt out of place in her brainy family. In fact, she's been sent back to repeat seventh grade (where she's done really well, by the way). Her grandmother, Mimi, was her real soulmate. Mimi lived with the Kishis. Even though her native language was Japanese and Claudia speaks only English, they communicated beautifully. Mimi helped Claudia realize how special she is. You see, Claudia has something no other Kishi has — an incredible talent for art. She can sculpt, draw, paint, and make gorgeous jewelry. You can tell she's an artist just by looking at her. She puts together the most striking outfits from clothes she buys at flea markets. At our meeting, for example, she was wearing an old-fashioned felt hat, a billowy button-down white shirt, a super-wide tie hand-painted with a Hawaiian sunset, cuffed khaki shorts, and brown-and-white bucks with knee-high white socks. I could never dream up an outfit like that.

Actually, art is not Claudia's only field of expertise. Junk food is, too. If she had the choice, she would live on candy, ice cream, and potato chips (the greasier the better). Of course, her parents permit only wholesome food in the house, so Claudia hides her junk food all over her room. She also has to hide her Nancy Drew books, because Mr. and Mrs. Kishi think they're not serious enough literature. (You know what I think? If Claudia's parents didn't forbid all that stuff, Claudia wouldn't crave it as much.)

Claudia sure doesn't look like a high-calorie-food addict. She's not an ounce overweight, and I've never seen a pimple on her face. Actually, she's quite stunning. Her hair is a silky jet black and her eyes are full of humor. I love her smile, too. It can lift you out of your worst mood.

Claudia, by the way, is the club vice-president. Her main duties are official meeting host, head of snacks, and club telephone supplier.

No, we don't stick Claudia with the whole phone bill. We contribute to it every month. That's where Stacey comes in. She's the club treasurer. Each Monday she collects dues from us, which she stores in an old manila envelope. At the end of the month she pays our bills. (Besides the phone, our main expense is gas money for Kristy's brother Charlie, who chauffeurs Kristy and Abby to meetings.) Stacey also makes sure to set aside funds for Kid-Kit supplies. Then, if enough cash is left over, we treat ourselves to something special, like a pizza party.

Stacey's the only BSC member with the patience for all those numbers. Math comes naturally to her. Recently she joined the middle school math team and she became the state scoring champ.

I know. You're picturing some kind of math nerd with bad hair and a calculator in each pocket. Well, don't. Stacey is proof that stereotypes are stupid. She's sophisticated and friendly. And as far as clothes go, you can predict the next *YM* cover just by looking at her outfits. She loves fashion. Lately her favorite styles are really angular and urban. Her favorite color is black, which looks striking against her blonde hair.

Looking at Stacey's wardrobe, you wouldn't be surprised she grew up in New York City, the fashion capital of the USA. She moved to Stoneybrook (and joined the BSC) after her dad's company transferred him to its Connecticut office. But then the company transferred him back, and Stacey became a New Yorker again. All the moving around took its toll on Mr. and Mrs. McGill, who hadn't been getting along well anyway. Soon they divorced, and Stacey was back in Stoneybrook, this time with just her mom.

Stacey weathered that crisis very well. It's a good thing she's so strong, because she is under doctors' orders to avoid stress. You see, she has a medical condition called diabetes. That means her body can't handle refined sugar. A nondiabetic's body has a kind of sorting system for sugar. Some is released slowly into the blood over time, some converted to energy, some stored as fat. In Stacey's case, all the sugar rushes right into the blood, which could cause serious problems. Fortunately Stacey can lead a normal life. She has to eat regular meals, stay away from sugary foods, and give herself daily injections of a hormone called insulin. (It used to make me queasy to think of that, but Stacey assures me it's pretty painless.)

Stacey is not the only BSC member from New York. She's also not the only one with a health condition. Abby qualifies on both counts. She grew up on Long Island, not far from the Big Apple. (I have to say "*on* Long Island"; Abby says "*in*" is wrong.) She also has asthma and major allergies. Her backpack always contains inhalers and lots of tissues.

Abby is our alternate member, which means she substitutes for any officer who misses a meeting. She took Dawn's place in the BSC. And just in time, too. After Dawn's move, we tried to get by with only six regular members, but we were swamped. Right around then, Abby moved to Stoneybrook with her mother and sister, two houses away from the Thomas/Brewers. When Kristy found that her new neighbors included twin girls our age — hallelujah!

Yes, Abby has a twin. Her name is Anna, and

she's a lot like me. She's quiet, thoughtful, and unathletic. I was hoping she'd join the BSC, too. We invited her, but she said she didn't have the time. She practices violin several hours every day. She's determined to become a professional musician.

For twins, the girls couldn't be less alike. Abby has zero interest in playing an instrument (except, perhaps, air guitar). She's a phenomenal natural athlete. Even her hair is different from Anna's. Well, it's the same color — dark brown, almost black. But Anna wears hers short and straight, with bangs, while Abby's is like a big hair fountain that cascades in ringlets around her face.

Abby is outgoing and full of jokes. She fit in to the BSC instantly. (If I had to do what she did, hopping into a club that had consisted of tight friends for so long, I'd have been petrified.) We've all become very close to her. She even invited us to her Bat Mitzvah ceremony. That's an extremely important rite that thirteen-year-old girls in the Jewish faith go through. It was so moving, especially when Abby and Anna recited in Hebrew from the Torah, the holy book of Judaism.

Lately, Abby's been psyched because at the end of the summer she'll be playing on a unified Special Olympics team. (She's already practicing!) It's sad that her dad won't be around to see it. He died in a car accident when she was nine. (I don't know the details. Abby doesn't like to talk about it, and we respect that.)

Now you know about our officers. Like Abby and Anna, we're all thirteen. And except for Claudia, we're in eighth grade.

Jessi and Mallory are our junior members. They're both eleven years old and in sixth grade. They do everything we do, with two exceptions: They don't have official duties at our meetings, and they don't baby-sit at night because their parents won't let them.

Both girls hate that no-night-sitting rule. They consider themselves victims of the "oldest-child syndrome" in their families. Jessi has a little sister and brother, and Mallory has seven younger siblings. According to Jessi and Mal, their parents let the younger ones do whatever they want.

To be fair, that's not entirely true. But they like to complain anyway. It's part of their bond, I guess. Jessi and Mal are absolute best friends. They're also the world's biggest horse-book fans. They know to the day when each *Saddle Club* book is going to arrive in the stores.

In certain ways, Mal and Jessi are very different. For one thing, Mal's white and Jessi's black. Mal has thick reddish-brown hair and wears glasses and braces. She's happiest when she's writing and illustrating her own stories. Jessi pulls her hair back into a tight bun and walks with the elegant grace of a dancer. She has taken ballet classes all her life, and she dreams of being in the American Ballet Theatre someday.

Junior or not, all regular BSC members are required to attend meetings and pay dues. Our two *associates,* however, don't. They help out when we're overloaded with jobs.

One of our associates is my boyfriend, Logan. He can't be a full-time member because he's involved in after-school sports. Logan is fantastic with kids. He also happens to be incredibly handsome: blue eyes, a dimply smile, and curly, light brown hair. He has a great sense of humor and he speaks with this wonderful hint of an accent he picked up from his hometown, Louisville, Kentucky.

(Okay, okay, I'll stop gushing. I can't help it.)

Our other associate is Shannon Kilbourne. She attends a private school called Stoneybrook Day School, and her schedule is pretty much packed with after-school activities. That day, for example, she was dying to see Dawn, but she had to go to a drama club rehearsal.

As for me, even an appointment with the President of the United States wouldn't have been more important than Dawn's first BSC meeting of the summer!

We were in Extreme Snack Mode, munching away on chips and Yodels. Dawn was leaning against Claudia's wall, happily chewing her molasses bread. "Looks like you guys regained your appetites," she remarked.

"Never lost them," Claudia said.

"*You* didn't," Kristy piped up. "After seeing that guy hurl that chunk of food, I thought I'd never eat again."

Stacey made a face. "Kristy, puh-*leeze*."

"Well, it's true," Kristy retorted. "It was pretty gross."

"I think that was the most scared I've ever been in my life," I said.

"Really?" Claudia asked skeptically.

"Sure. I thought he was going to die in front of us."

"I knew he'd be okay," Claudia said. "I've been much more scared than that."

"When?" Stacey asked.

"Crossing a street in New York City," Claudia answered. "No, not really. It was when Mimi had her stroke, I guess. That was the first time I realized she wasn't going to live forever." She sighed deeply. "How about you, Stace?"

Stacey thought a moment. "The time in New York when my diabetes got out of control and I ended up in the hospital. I thought *I* was going to die."

"My scariest moment was when my dad was laid off from his job," Mallory volunteered. "I was sure I'd end up in an orphanage like Oliver Twist."

"For me it was that car accident with Aunt Cecelia," Jessi said, "and seeing my little brother all limp in the backseat. I'm still so grateful every time I see him jumping around the house now."

"My parents' divorce," Dawn spoke up. "I kind of knew it might happen, but when it did, I went into shock."

Abby was munching away, looking very thoughtful.

"How about you?" I asked her.

Right away I wished I could reel in those words. Abby's face clouded over. "My dad's accident," she said softly.

"Sorry," I said. "I didn't mean to — "

Abby smiled. "It's all right, Mary Anne."

Stacey said quickly, "Well, thank goodness Sharon saved the day."

"That guy was lucky," Kristy added.

"You know what bothers me?" I asked. "What if Sharon hadn't been there?"

"Mary Anne, that's morbid," Dawn replied.

"I'm serious. Who would have saved that man? I mean, none of us tried."

"I've never really done that Henrick thing," Claudia remarked.

"Heimlich," Kristy corrected her.

"I saw a poster about it in the cafeteria," Mallory said. "But it was near the bathrooms."

"I've seen that poster a million times," Abby said. "But it kind of goes in one eye and out the other."

"I know the basic idea, but not enough to try it," Kristy remarked. "I guess you only learn stuff like that by practicing."

"How?" Stacey asked. "By hanging out in restaurants and asking people to choke?"

"Classes," Kristy said. "You take a first-aid class."

"Stoneybrook Community Center gives them," Jessi said. "My mom took one when our family signed up for the pool."

That sounded like a great idea. "Can kids our age take it?"

"I'll find out," Jessi said.

Kristy sat forward. "We should *all* take it! You're right, Mary Anne. We were totally unprepared. Think of what would happen if one of our charges started choking like that man did. Or if some worse accident happens and we need to give mouth-to-mouth resuscitation. Would any of us know how to do that?"

We all just sat there, too ashamed to say no.

"If the SCC gives a first-aid class, I move that the entire BSC take it," Kristy announced. "All in favor?"

"AYE!" It was unanimous.

I was excited. Things were going to change. I was going to de-chicken myself.

From this moment on, Mary Anne the Meek would be a thing of the past.

I think it was the photo of the sliced-up heart on the wall that got me. Or the one of a man performing CPR on an unconscious baby.

Or maybe it was the fact that Alan Gray, the most obnoxious boy in the eighth grade, had signed up for the Basic Life Support for Teens class at the Stoneybrook Community Center.

Whatever it was, I was feeling ill.

Our instructor was a young, dark-haired woman dressed in shorts, running shoes, and a chambray shirt tied at the waist. It took all the concentration I had to focus on her. I was afraid I would faint.

All the feelings I had had at the airport cafeteria were rushing back in, even though the incident had happened four days before. And I realized they were the same feelings I have when I see a violent movie or a gruesome newscast.

Fear. Nausea. Stomachache.

I hate violence. Seeing people in pain makes my heart stop. I can't stand the sight of blood. I can't stand the *thought* of blood.

Basic Life Support for Teens was four sessions long. It was going to cover every horrible thing that could possibly occur. The course description mentioned choking, heart attacks, drowning, knife wounds, snake bites, and head trauma.

Why was I doing this to myself?

I looked around. About fifteen kids were taking the class. Kristy, Stacey, and Claudia were deep in conversation. Jessi, Mallory, and Dawn were cracking up over an imitation that Abby was doing. Alan Gray was goofing off with his friends Pete Black and Irv Hirsch.

Logan had told me he'd be coming to the class, but he was nowhere to be seen. Which was too bad. If he were there, I'd feel calmer.

"Hello, I'm Shelley Golden," announced the instructor.

"Hello, I'm Alan Gray," chirped Alan.

"I'm Pete Black," said Pete.

"And I'm Little Boy Blue," muttered Irv.

Well, they thought that was the funniest exchange ever spoken. They were laughing so hard, they sounded like braying mules.

"How long have they been practicing *that* one?" Stacey murmured.

Boy, were we off to a bad start. Of all the

first-aid classes and all the time periods to take them, why did we have to choose the same one as Alan Gray?

Shelley Golden was fixing the three boys with a hard stare. Then she smiled slyly and cleared her throat.

"You know," she said, "I recommend you boys apply your *gray* matter to this course, because someday, when one of you is *black* and *blue,* you'll all be sorry you missed a *golden* opportunity."

"All riiiight!" Abby said, bursting into applause.

Alan and friends sank into their chairs.

Shelley Golden was quick. I already knew I liked her.

"Now, before we start," she went on, "I insist you call me Shelley. And ask as many questions as you want. When it comes to first-aid preparedness, no question is stupid."

I could see Alan itching to prove her wrong, but he kept a lid on it.

"How many of you know about the Firefighters' Fair at the end of this month?" Shelley asked.

Most of us raised our hands. The Firefighter's Fair is an annual Stoneybrook event. It's basically a big town festival given by the fire department.

"Well, the fair has really increased fire-safety

awareness in Stoneybrook," Shelley said. "I think we can do the same for first-aid awareness. I'm part of a committee that has proposed a Stoneybrook Safety Day, and if it's approved, I'd like to involve all of you to it. So pay attention."

Gulp. That was the last thing I'd want to do. Performing Heimlich maneuvers and mouth-to-mouth resuscitation in public? Forget it.

"Anyway, first things first," Shelley continued. "I'm assuming, since you're all teenagers, that most of your personal contacts include friends, siblings, and cousins."

"And charges!" Kristy blurted out. "Uh, I mean, kids we baby-sit for."

"Exactly," Shelley said. "So a good portion of our first class will be basic pediatric safety. I happen to be a certified CPR instructor, so we'll cover some of that, too."

"Can Alan practice mouth-to-mouth with Kristy?" Irv asked.

"Gag me!" Kristy cried.

"Only if she agrees," Shelley said pleasantly. "Otherwise, you, Irving, may be his partner."

Now the whole class cracked up. Irv's face turned tomato red.

"Do you really have to, like, put your lips on the other person?" asked a blonde girl I didn't know.

"Do they make lip cootie protectors?" someone else asked.

"If and when the time comes," Shelley replied, "and I hope it never does, you will not have the slightest hesitation — man, boy, girl, woman. I have seen someone perform CPR on his pet dog."

A major "EEEEWWWWW!" rang out in the room.

"But CPR is an involved technique," Shelley said, "for use in extreme emergencies. Using it properly and knowing *when* to use it are absolutely crucial. I'll teach you the basics, but I strongly recommend that someday you take the CPR course I give."

Alan whispered something to his friends and they giggled. (I guess they knew better than to goof off aloud.)

Shelley reached into a file cabinet drawer and pulled out a handful of objects, including a pacifier, a calculator, a deflated balloon, a fake daisy and a fake poinsettia, a plastic bunch of grapes, and a plastic hot dog. "Some common household objects. Pretend all the plastic ones are real. Now, how many are dangerous?"

"None of them," said Pete.

"The pacifier has a mouth guard that's been designed to be larger than babies' mouths," Kristy announced, "so they can't swallow it."

"Until they chew through the latex nipple," Shelley said. "Then it can break off and become lodged in their throats. You must always check for cracks. How about the flowers?"

"The pot could crack open their head," Abby volunteered.

"True," Shelley replied. "But I was thinking of the plant itself. See, some plants, like poinsettias, are poisonous. Others, like daisies and dandelions, aren't — not that you should *feed* them to little children."

"Some honey and dandelions on your rice cereal, sweetie?" said Alan in a squeaky voice.

Kristy gave him a killer Look.

"I will give you a list of harmful and harmless plants," Shelley said. "Now, how about the calculator?"

"Uh, a kid could bite off the buttons?" guessed a girl in the front row.

"Not likely," Shelley said. "But the battery is a disk shape and, besides being poisonous, could become lodged in the throat." Shelley held up the hot dog. "This one?"

"Safe!" Pete shouted like a baseball umpire. "You just cut it up into sections."

"Those sections," Shelley said, "are just about the exact diameter of a child's throat. They can plug it up tight, cutting off all air. Similar problem with grapes. And both of them can *hydrate,* meaning they expand as they become wet with saliva. The best method? Cut grapes in half and slice the hot dog in half lengthwise before cutting it into sections. Any questions? Okay, moving on to the balloon — "

"Very dangerous," Kristy interrupted. "The rubber can block off the air. In the BSC we keep balloons up high and throw out broken balloon pieces."

"My hero," Alan squeaked.

"Then we hide them in Alan Gray's sandwich," Abby muttered.

"Which leads to the next question," Shelley continued. "What do you do when a child at the table begins coughing on a piece of trapped food?"

"Oooh! Oooh!" shouted a boy in the back, waving his hand in the air. "The Heinlein maneuver!"

"Heimlich," Claudia confidently corrected him.

"Good guess, but no," Shelley replied. "If the child is coughing, that means the air passage is open. The cough should eventually clear the problem. Trying the Heimlich maneuver in that case would do more harm than good. What does a person sound like when the air passage is blocked?"

I knew the answer to that. The man in the cafeteria was still fresh in my mind. "Silent," I said.

"Exactly. No air, no sound. If this ever happens to you, attract attention and begin pointing to your throat. It's possible to give yourself the Heimlich maneuver but it's much more preferable for someone else to. Now, before I teach you the maneuver, who knows where your diaphragm is?"

No answer.

"Point to the center of your collarbone," Shelley went on. "Then slide your finger down the center of your chest until it reaches the very bottom of your ribs. The diaphragm is inside that spot, stretching from the front to the back of your body, like the head of a drum. That is what pushes the air out when you exhale." Now Shelley began walking down the aisle toward us. "I need a volunteer. Alan, would you please stand up?"

"Me?" Alan asked.

"Oooooooh," said Pete and Irv.

(Honestly, they are so immature.)

Slowly and sheepishly Alan rose to his feet. Shelley turned him around so that she was facing his back. Then she wrapped her arms around him.

I thought some of the boys in the class were going to hyperventilate, they were laughing so hard.

"Calm down," Shelley said with a smile. "I am going to pretend Alan is choking and give him the Heimlich maneuver. First, I locate the diaphragm and clasp my fists together in front of it."

"Is this going to hurt?" Alan whimpered.

"Only if you laugh," Shelley replied.

As she began Heimlich-ing Alan, I noticed Logan walking into class and sitting in a seat by the door. I smiled and waved.

Logan smiled back. Sort of. He seemed pre-occupied.

I am such a worrywart. Right away I thought something terrible had happened. I was dying to ask him what was going on (if anything).

When Shelley asked us to pick partners in order to practice the Heimlich maneuver, I moved toward Logan, but someone nearer to him beat me to the punch.

After guiding us through the technique, Shelley discussed other basic first aid topics. Most of it was stuff we BSC members already knew about, such as bee stings, nosebleeds, stomachaches, and fevers. She stressed the need to call 911 for worse emergencies. And she managed to keep Alan and his gang meek and obedient. I took notes and enjoyed the class a lot, but I was anxious to talk to Logan.

"As you know, our next class is Friday," Shelley announced at the end of the period, "so be here same time, two o'clock. We'll discuss CPR. See you then!"

Everyone in class stood up and started gabbing at once. I quickly made my way across the room toward Logan.

"Hi!" I said. "Are you all right?"

"Yeah," Logan replied. "Fine."

He sure didn't sound fine. His voice was soft and clipped. And he wasn't looking me in the eye. He just walked out into the hallway.

"Are you sure?" I persisted, following behind him.

"Um, let's go outside," Logan said. "I need to tell you something."

Now I was really worried. I did not like the sound of this.

"Mary Anne?" Dawn's voice called from behind me.

I turned and said, "I have to talk to Logan. I'll try not to be long."

"No problem, take your time," Dawn called back. "I'll meet you at home."

Logan was already pushing his way through a side exit. I jogged after him. We emerged into the warm afternoon sunlight in an isolated corner of the Stoneybrook Community Center parking lot.

Logan slumped silently against the wall. His eyes were moist.

My heart was thumping like a jackhammer. I fought back tears. "What?" was all I could manage to say.

Logan swallowed deeply. A tear trickled down his cheek and he quickly turned and brushed it away, as if he were just scratching an itch.

Horrible thoughts shot through my brain.

He's seeing another girl.

A high school girl.

A college girl.

Maybe someone has died.

No, his family's moving. That has to be it.

My knees were shaking. I tried to look Logan in the eye, but tears were clouding the view.

"Mary Anne," he said, his voice cracking, "I need to tell you something very important. And you're not going to like it."

CHAPTER 4

"My dad," Logan said, "wants me to go to boarding school."

Whaaaat?

That came out of left field. Completely.

The first thing I felt was a sudden surge of relief.

No accidents. No deaths. We weren't breaking up.

Then the news sank in. "You mean, like a sleepaway school?"

"You live there the whole school year. Like college." Logan took a deep breath. "It's the same school Dad went to. He says he spent the best years of his life there. It's called Conant Academy, and it's way out in the woods in New Hampshire."

"But — but I thought he grew up in the South!"

"He did. That's the point, Mary Anne. It's *boarding* school. All the kids are from far away."

"But why? What's wrong with Stoney-brook?"

Logan shrugged. "I don't know. I guess Dad thinks if I don't go to a prep school I won't get into a good enough college or something. He says the competition is tougher at Conant. It'll sharpen my mind."

"But — but you don't want to do it," I said. "Do you?"

"Are you kidding? But what am I supposed to do? Dad already paid a deposit."

My stomach was turning inside out. The idea of living in a dorm with strange kids at our age was weird enough. But Logan? Leaving home for good?

I was speechless.

I kept looking at Logan's eyes. Sometimes he likes to concoct ridiculous stories, just to see if I'll believe them. Then the corners of his eyes crinkle and he begins to crack up.

But he was totally uncrinkly and uncracking.

"That's not even the worst part," Logan continued, his voice tightening with anger. "He also wants me to spend a month in some . . . some boot camp!"

"The army?" I blurted out. "But you're thirteen!"

"Not that kind of boot camp. That's just what I call it. It's really a survival camp — Survival and Leadership Training Seminars, or something like that. Dad did that when he was a kid, too. He says it builds character. You do calisthenics and run a million miles and climb rocks and carry heavy stuff up mountains until you're practically dead. Then you have to learn to survive in the wilderness without food or shelter, eating berries and stuff."

"They're allowed to let a kid do that? What about all the bears and foxes?"

"You punch them in the nose, I guess, because you have so much character by then," Logan said with a shrug. "I don't know. I mean, to tell you the truth, the outdoors part sounds cool. But that only happens the last couple of days. The rest is three and a half weeks of boredom."

"And then you come home and pack up to leave again," I added.

"Exactly. It doesn't make any sense. Besides, I have stuff I want to do *here*. Mr. Fee is expecting me to work at the Rosebud. And I just found out I'm supposed to be the starting shortstop on my summer league baseball team."

Logan was so upset he was pacing, clenching and unclenching his fists. I desperately wanted to make him feel better.

But I felt as if I'd been hit over the head.

I'd been looking forward to a nice, relaxing

summer — baby-sitting, hanging out with Dawn and my friends, going out with Logan. Now Logan was going to be plucked away, never to be seen in Stoneybrook again.

"What's going to happen to us in September?" I asked.

"Lots of visits, I guess," Logan said gloomily. "If there are roads that go all the way to Conant. It's in the middle of nowhere."

"Look, um, you shouldn't worry too much," I said, trying to sound upbeat. "Maybe your dad will reconsider."

Logan gave a snorting kind of laugh. "Right. You know the way he is."

"You guys must have had a huge argument."

"Sort of. I was mostly shocked. Dad kept saying stuff like, 'You won't know if you like it until you try it,' and 'Someday you'll thank me for this.' "

Now Shelley Golden was walking across the parking lot, fishing for keys in her shoulder bag.

"Let's get out of here, Mary Anne," Logan said, "before she sees us blubbering."

"My house, okay? We can talk more there."

"Just promise me one thing. We don't talk to anyone about this."

"Sure, okay," I agreed.

Logan and I walked around the corner of the

building to the bike rack. We didn't say much on the ride home. Both of us were a little shell-shocked.

When we arrived, Dawn was alone in the kitchen, eating a salad. I could hear Jeff in the backyard, playing with the Pike triplets. "Hi, guys!" Dawn called out.

"I'm sorry, Dawn," I said, "I didn't mean to walk out on you after class."

"Hey, you're allowed to sneak off with your boyfriend. These things are important." Dawn raised a knowing eyebrow.

Logan and I must have looked like the twin masks of doom, because her smile vanished. "Uh-oh. You didn't break up, did you?"

I smiled cheerfully. I tried to laugh. "No way."

"Then why do you both look like curdled cheese?" Dawn asked.

"It's just the heat," Logan replied.

"Right," Dawn said skeptically. "Okay, keep secrets from me. I don't mind. I'm only your sister."

Logan took a deep breath and sat down. "Dawn, this is not to go past this table, okay?"

He went through the details again. Dawn listened closely, her brows scrunching together with every painful sentence.

"Wow," she said after he'd finished. "That's bad. Listen, can I make you some bancha tea?"

"Some what?" Logan asked.

"Tea from the bark of a bancha tree," Dawn explained. "It's very soothing."

"No thanks," Logan replied. "Do you have any Yoo Hoo or Mountain Dew?"

Dawn looked as if he had just asked for sewer water. "I hope not."

I went to the fridge and took out the only soft drink in there, seltzer with natural raspberry flavor.

"When did your dad tell you all this, Logan?" Dawn asked.

"Today."

I poured seltzer for us all. "And your mom?" I asked. "Does she want you to go, too?"

"I can't tell," Logan answered. "I think she's trying to make up her mind."

"That's good," Dawn said. "That means the problem is still fresh. If you push hard enough, you have a chance."

Logan shook his head. "But you know my dad. He just digs in. When I told him about summer baseball, he said, 'Conant has the best baseball team in its league.' Then I asked him what was wrong with Stoneybrook schools and he said, 'They're not the best. A Conant boy has a jump start on the rest of the world.' "

Dawn made a face. "He really said that? 'A Conant boy'?"

"You mean, Conant isn't — " I began.

"Coed?" Logan jumped in. "Nope. That's the other horrible thing. I really put up a fight about that." Logan suddenly turned red and gave me a guilty look. "Not that I — I don't mean to — it's just that, you know, I'm not used to *not* going to school with girls, that's all."

"I think your mom is the key," Dawn insisted. "Work on her, and she'll work on him."

"It's not like that in my family, Dawn," Logan snapped. "Everything is right out in the open. Dad says he and Mom talked about the decision a lot. Don't you see? It's a done deal. If I thought I could do something about it, I wouldn't be moping around here." He swigged down his seltzer and stood up. "Thanks for the drink, Mary Anne. I — I have to go help Mom with Hunter. See you."

With that, he left the kitchen. I followed him to the front door and said good-bye. Standing at the door, I watched him until he disappeared around the corner.

He looked the way I felt.

Totally destroyed.

Wednesday

I learned quite a few things today.

One. The Hobart boys have very hard heads.

Two. There are no traffic rules on Mars.

Three. Jackie Rodowsky needs more than a bike helmet. Body armor, I'm afraid, is the only hope. . . .

"But — but — I'm scared!" cried Mathew Hobart. His knuckles were practically white as he clutched the handlebar of his bike, wobbling down the sidewalk along the Carle Playground.

"Of course you are," Abby said sympathetically. She was jogging alongside Mathew, holding the back of his seat. "It's normal."

One of Mathew's older brothers, James, circled gracefully around them on his ten-speed bike. "Just pretend the training wheels are still on!" he shouted.

"I'm trying!" Mathew retorted. "Who-o-o-oa! Don't let go, Abby!"

"I won't!" Abby said.

"I'm bored!" whined James. "Can I ride to Buddy's house?"

RRRRRRRRRRRR . . . whirred the engine noise of Johnny Hobart's tricycle behind them. "Hey! Wait!" he shouted.

Actually, it sounded more like, "Hi! White!" You see, the Hobarts are from Australia. They have great accents. (Wonderful expressions, too, such as "brecky" for "breakfast." One day I heard them talk about "firing up the barbie," and I thought they were going to set fire to a doll. Boy, was I wrong. "Barbie" means "barbecue.")

James Hobart is eight, Mathew is six, and

Johnny's four. They have an older brother, Ben, who's eleven. (He sometimes baby-sits, but he was shopping for sleepaway camp supplies with his mom that day.) All four have red hair and freckles. They look so much alike, you'd think they were quadruplets stuck in different parts of a time warp.

On Wednesday, Abby had a big project in mind: Operation Mathew on Wheels. Ever since his parents took off his training wheels, he'd been struggling to ride a two-wheeler. Abby was determined to teach him once and for all.

Mathew picked up speed. Abby sensed that he had his balance. As gently as she could, she let go. Mathew was doing it!

"Abby's not holding you!" James sang out.

Abby could see Mathew's body freeze up in panic.

Mathew wobbled. Immediately he pushed his leg backward and braked. Abby had been keeping pace alongside him. She nearly took the handlebar in her stomach.

Somehow she managed to jump away. Mathew wasn't so lucky. His bike fell out from under him. He hit the ground, helmet-first.

"Ow-ow-ow-ow!" he moaned, rolling on the grass.

Abby ran to help him up. "Are you all right?"

"No!" Mathew replied, bursting into tears. "Why did you take me out on this stupid bike? I'll never ever *ever* learn how to ride it. I *hate* bikes!"

Abby wrapped him in a hug. "Hey, that's okay. We can take a rest from it. You were doing fine. Did I ever tell you what happened to me when I first tried — "

"Beebeebeebeebeep! Coming in for a landing from Mars!" yelled Johnny as he pedaled closer.

Crash! Right into Mathew's bike.

Johnny burst out laughing. "Traffic jam, traffic jelly!"

"Hey, stop that!" Mathew cried out.

James had taken one lap around the playground and was zooming by. "Are you still falling down, you big baby?" he taunted Mathew.

"I'm resting!" Mathew retorted.

"No, he falled!" Johnny insisted.

"Did not, tattletale!" Mathew yelled.

James was looking over his shoulder at his brothers. He was zigzagging lazily toward the playground entrance.

Out of the corner of her eye, Abby spotted two nannies heading out of the playground. They were deep in conversation, wheeling two babies who were fast asleep in their strollers.

"James, watch out!" Abby yelled.

James faced forward. His bike swerved toward the babies.

The nannies gasped. They tried to yank the strollers back.

James was moving too fast to turn away. He jammed on the brakes and skidded.

In a moment, James and his bike were both tumbling to the ground. James's helmet thudded against the dirt.

Abby sped toward him. "Did you hurt yourself?"

"Did I hit the — ?" James sprang to his feet and glanced at the nannies. He seemed more embarrassed than injured. "Sorry," he murmured.

"You need to watch where you're going!" one of them snapped.

As the two women walked away, Mathew grinned at his older brother. "*Now* who's the big baby?"

"Yeah!" said Johnny, crashing his trike into James's bike. "Traffic jam, traffic jelly!"

"Sto-o-op!" yelled James.

"I'm from Mars," Johnny explained. "We don't have grabbity."

"Uh, guys," Abby said wearily, "maybe we should try this another time."

"No!" all three said at the same time.

"Hiiiii!" called a voice from behind them.

They all turned to see Jackie Rodowsky riding toward them on his Stingray bike.

Abby's heart jumped. Jackie is known as the Walking Disaster. He's only seven, but he's had enough accidents to last a lifetime — including a crash into a tree on his bike. Unfortunately he hadn't been wearing a helmet at the time, and he had to be hospitalized with a concussion.

This time, Jackie was wearing his helmet. He was wearing elbow and knee guards, too. He was riding slowly, on the far right-hand side of the street. Just before he turned into a driveway to mount the sidewalk, he gave a hand signal. He was all smiles.

Abby sighed with relief. "Now, you see how careful Jackie is when he rides?"

But Jackie's smile had vanished. His legs had stopped pumping, too.

Abby heard a rip. Jackie was wobbling jerkily from side to side.

She caught a glimpse of Jackie's pants, caught in his bike chain.

"Who-o-oa!" Jackie toppled over, hitting the ground with a soft thud.

"Ja-a-ackieeee!" shouted James and Mathew, cracking up. (I know, how cruel.)

Jackie was gazing at his ankle in bewilderment as Abby sprinted to his side. "What happened?" he murmured.

Quickly Abby extracted his torn pants from the chain. "Can you move your ankle?"

"Uh-huh," Jackie answered, flexing his foot. "Good thing I remembered my helmet, huh?"

Abby smiled. "Next time, try some ankle clips."

The Hobart boys were right behind her now, still giggling. "Wacky Jackie," James muttered.

"Ahem," Abby said. "You guys aren't exactly in the running for the Safe Biker of the Year award, either."

"I am, traffic jam!" Johnny sang.

"At least we don't get our pants caught up in our chains," James said.

"That's just because you're wearing shorts," Jackie reminded him.

"Look," Abby interrupted, "you're all good riders, okay? Just keep remembering to use your safety rules."

"On Mars, there are no safety rules," Johnny insisted.

"You mean, like, hand signals and stuff?" James asked, ignoring his little brother. "Nobody does that. It's dorky."

"Is wearing a helmet dorky?" Abby asked.

"No way!" Jackie piped up.

"Kids used to think so, when helmets were first introduced," Abby said. "See, it's not about dorky and nondorky. It's about smart and stupid."

"I use signals," Jackie said. "One time a driver even thanked me."

"When I was a kid," Abby explained, "my dad always told me to watch out for people in parked cars. He said it so many times I wanted to barf. Then one day I was speeding down a big hill near my house. I was just about to come to this busy intersection, and I had the green light. *Nyyyeeearr* — I zoomed as fast as I could. A red sportscar was parked at the curb, and just out of habit, I glanced into the car through its window. I could see a driver leaning into the door, ready to open it. I must have been going about thirty miles an hour as the door swung open — and I was heading right for him!"

"Did you die?" Johnny asked.

"Nope, I swung right around him and made the light," Abby replied. "But my heart was beating so hard, I could practically see my shirt move. And I never, ever complained about my dad's lecture again."

"Wow," Mathew murmured.

The kids all started talking at once. But Abby wasn't really listening. She was thinking about her dad. About how his advice had saved her life.

And about how she couldn't save his.

Right there, in front of the Carle Playground,

she realized that she had a duty. She needed to pass on what her dad had given her.

In the distance, Abby could see Jake Kuhn, Buddy Barrett, and Lindsey DeWitt heading toward them. Riding their bikes the wrong way on a one-way street.

Visions of Shelley Golden popped into her head. Abby thought about the upcoming Firefighters' Fair. If first aid and fire safety could be made so cool, why couldn't bike safety?

"Hiii!" the newcomers yelled as they approached.

Abby looked at her watch. Ben and his mom weren't due back at the Hobarts' for an hour or so. "Guys, you are all in luck," she announced. "Today is Stoneybrook Road Safety Day, and you are the lucky participants!"

James looked at her, dumbfounded. Buddy was ready to turn and bike away.

But Abby was already running through all the safety rules she knew, planning how to teach them.

And thinking of an appropriate reward.

"And whoever can master the Stevenson Rules of the Road exam will receive, free of charge, a three-scoop ice-cream sundae!"

"YEEAAAA!"

It was official. Abby was in business.

"I'll write," Logan said as we walked into the Stoneybrook Community Center parking lot.

"Uh-huh," I replied. "Me, too."

I could just picture it. Trudging home from school through the December snow and taking the letter out of the mailbox. *Dear Mary Anne, I meant to write in September but things have been busy here . . .*

"We can e-mail each other," Logan went on as we locked up our bikes. "I mean, if Dad allows me to go on-line at Conant. He might not. He's kind of old-fashioned that way. And I don't know the school policy, either, really."

I had visions of stern schoolmarms and mean priests, like the ones in *Jane Eyre* or *A Little Princess*. I could see them giving Logan the cold stare as he asked about computers, then handing him a quill pen.

"Do they have telephones there?" I asked.

Logan burst out laughing. "It's a prep school, Mary Anne, not a time machine."

"Well, you said it was way out in the woods. I just thought it might be one of those back-to-nature places."

"It's on a campus. Roads go to it. So do telephone wires and cables. If it weren't modern, nobody would want to enroll. Well, maybe Dawn would."

"Dawn's modern, Logan," I retorted.

"Hey, it was just a joke. Don't be so sensitive."

I shut my mouth. I did not think I was being too sensitive. What was I supposed to do? Be happy that Logan was going away? Kiss our relationship good-bye? Or was I supposed to wait patiently for his visits? Goodness knows I already had practice with that. I wait for Dawn's visits. I wait for Dad whenever he's on his business trips.

"Did you have a chance to talk to your mom?" I asked.

"About what?"

"Everything — the prep school, the boot camp. You know, the way Dawn suggested."

Logan rolled his eyes. "Dawn means well. But she doesn't know my parents."

"So you didn't talk to her?"

"Why should I? She just does whatever Dad says."

"That's not true, Logan. I've seen your mom and dad disagree."

We were approaching Stoneybrook Community Center now. Alan and his friends were hanging out by the front door, glancing at us and whispering.

Logan let out an exasperated sigh. "I'll talk to her if it makes you happy, okay?"

"Me?" I said. "What about you? You sound as if you *want* to go away."

"Can we please stop arguing?" Logan hissed.

My eyes were welling up. I hate hate *hate* fighting.

I wished Dawn had walked with us. She'd stayed back to wait for Stacey and Claudia, figuring Logan and I needed time to talk. Maybe if she'd come along, the conversation wouldn't have been so tense.

"Logan and Mary Anne sitting in a tree," Alan sang out.

"Grow up," Logan snapped, barging past Alan and into the building.

I followed behind, trying to ignore Alan's immature giggling. I spotted Kristy, Abby, Jessi, and Mallory near a trophy display. Kristy waved me over.

"What's with Logan?" she asked.

"He had . . . uh, a fight with his dad," I replied. (Well, it was sort of the truth.)

"We made it!" called Stacey's voice from behind us.

I turned to see her, Claudia, and Dawn walking across the lobby. "Sorry we're so late," Dawn said.

"Stacey had a crisis," Claudia said. "She called me frantically, right before we were supposed to leave. I had to perform emergency hair support."

"I must have slept on it funny," Stacey explained.

"It was awful," Claudia went on. "Broken, twisted, and lifeless. I was crying. I didn't think we'd make it. I figured it would be a hat day. But we pulled through!"

"See?" Stacey said, fluffing out her hair.

"Looks the same as always," Kristy said.

Claudia curtsied. "Thank you!"

"Uh, guys?" Abby said, pointing to her watch. "Class?"

We were off and running. We made it to class just as Alan and his friends slouched in. Shelley Golden was sitting at her desk, busily shuffling papers. Logan had taken a seat by the window and was staring glumly into the parking lot. He gave me a tight, distracted half smile as I sat nearby.

Shelley Golden, on the other hand, was beaming. "Okay, listen up!" she cried out. "I have some great news. Remember my proposal about a Stoneybrook Safety Day? Well, actually, it wasn't *my* proposal. I was representing the Stoneybrook Emergency Service Council, which is comprised of police officers, fire fighters, emergency-room service technicians, doctors, and nurses. Anyway, our idea was approved! The mayor has decided to make next Saturday and Sunday Stoneybrook Safety Weekend. Sunday for the Firefighters' Fair, and Saturday for the First Annual Stoneybrook Safety Day. And I expect all of you to be our first victims."

"Cool," said Abby. "I'll go."

"I'm serious about the victim part," Shelley said. "We are going to stage a mock disaster, and we need volunteers — people who will pretend to have broken legs or be sick or — "

"How about food poisoning?" Alan asked. "I can barf on cue."

"Ew, gross, Alan!" Stacey cried out.

"Thank you," Alan replied.

Shelley laughed. "Alan, you will be our star victim."

"Yyyyesss!" Kristy shouted.

"My other news," Shelley said, "is that I've obtained permission for us to visit the Stoneybrook General Hospital emergency room during our class next Tuesday. That should be very informative."

Informative? My stomach was churning just thinking about it.

"Today," Shelley went on, "I'm going to begin with a brief CPR demonstration."

She reached into a closet and pulled out a realistic-looking baby doll. Gently she lay it facedown on her desk. "We'll start with infants. What do you do if a baby is unconscious, completely unresponsive?"

I felt a catch in my throat. I thought of all the baby BSC charges — Jessi's brother, Squirt; Andrea Prezzioso; Lucy Newton. What would I do if something happened to them?

Cry, probably.

"Tap the baby's back?" a girl asked.

"Blow into her mouth?" Mallory guessed.

Shelley shook her head. "Shout, 'Help!' If there are any people within hearing distance, make one of them call nine-one-one. That is the cardinal rule. CPR is difficult. If it's done wrong, it's potentially dangerous. Next step, turn the baby onto its back, trying to treat its body as one unit."

Lifting the doll's left arm, Shelley turned the body over gently, cradling it in her left forearm and holding its head.

"It's best if you do this on a hard surface. Now, try to open the airway by lifting the chin and moving back the forehead until the mouth is just barely open. Then, look, listen, and feel. *Look* for chest movement, *listen* for breathing, and move your cheek close to the mouth to *feel* for breath."

Shelley demonstrated. I could hardly see her for the tears in my eyes. The poor little doll looked so limp and lifeless.

Around me, I could hear a few shuddering breaths. The kind you make when you're trying not to cry. I wasn't the only one upset.

"If the baby is not breathing," Shelley continued, "then you begin CPR while you're waiting for the ambulance. First you give two rescue breaths. With a baby, you can actually put your mouth around both the nose and the mouth. Be sure to make an airtight seal. Then blow twice, making sure to watch the baby's chest."

Shelley blew once, and the baby's chest rose.

It looked so realistic. Sort of like Lucy Newton.

A lot like Lucy Newton.

I began to feel faint. I grabbed the edge of my desk.

"Mary Anne?" Kristy called out.

Logan bolted up and ran to my side. He knelt beside me and asked, "Are you okay?"

"Fine," I said.

All around me, I could hear chairs scraping on the floor. From the front of the class came the sound of Shelley's second rescue breath.

"Emergency!" Abby's voice called out.

"I'm fine!" I insisted.

I must have looked awful. Kids were crowding around me. Claudia began fanning me with looseleaf paper. Shelley was running toward me, too, leaving the baby on the table.

I felt like such a fool.

Why couldn't I have been born with a stronger stomach? Not to mention a braver heart.

Mary Anne the Chicken strikes again.

"I don't know what you're worried about, Mary Anne," Dawn said, gulping down a spoonful of whole-grain cereal. "Emergency rooms are interesting. At least they seem that way on TV."

"Lots of blood and guts," Jeff added.

I stared at my bowl. It might as well have contained slugs with garlic. "I don't feel well."

I pushed the bowl aside. I was nauseous. I was shaky. I wanted to go back to sleep for the rest of the day.

The last thing I wanted to do was go to an emergency room.

Tigger, my kitten, climbed into my lap. I think he could sense how awful I was feeling.

I had been dreading Tuesday morning for four whole days. I could hardly sleep the night before. I kept dreaming about a body being wheeled down a long, white corridor. Somehow, in my dream, I was hovering over the body. Then I zoomed in close to realize it was . . . *me.*

"You're just grossed out, that's all," Dawn said. "I feel the same way every time I see a pork chop."

"Dawn, I couldn't even watch Shelley give that doll mouth-to-mouth resuscitation," I said. "How am I supposed to deal with a real, live emergency room?"

"You were fine after the initial shock," Dawn reminded me. "And anyway, we were all kind of shaken up. That little dummy looked so real."

Sharon poked her head into the kitchen. " 'Morning! Did either of you see my tennis shoes?"

"Where did you last wear them?" Dawn asked.

"I believe I took them off in here last night," Sharon replied.

Jeff darted around the kitchen, looking in the dishwasher, the refrigerator . . .

Dawn thought for a moment, then opened the pots-and-pans cupboard and fished out a pair of white New Balances.

"Ah," Sharon said. "Thanks."

I couldn't help laughing. Typical, forgetful Sharon. It amazed me that someone so spacey could have been so sharp during an emergency.

"Tell Mary Anne the emergency-room visit won't be so horrible," Dawn said.

"*Boring* is the word I would use," Sharon said. "The last time I had to go to one, I spent about six hours watching TV in the waiting room."

"Nothing disgusting happened?" I asked.

"Well, one teenage kid came in with a big, red rope burn on his arm, but he seemed pretty proud of that," Sharon replied. "The rest were just colds and stomachaches and nosebleeds. I found out that a lot of people go to the emergency room for ordinary problems."

"That's stupid," commented Jeff.

"Mary Anne, you can't run away from your fear," Dawn said. "The Tibetan Buddhists say that you have to *face* that fear, like a tiger."

"The who?" I asked.

Dawn shrugged. "My friend Maggie knows a few in L.A."

"Tigers?" Sharon asked.

"No, Tibetan Buddhists."

Tigger shifted his position in my lap. I ran my hand along his striped fur.

Like a tiger. That was exactly how I needed to be. I could stand stomachaches and nosebleeds and colds. Besides, if I stayed home, I would feel so ashamed of myself.

Not to mention the fact that I'd be missing

one of my last chances to be with Logan before he disappeared.

"Okay," I said. "I'll go. But if I start to faint, catch me."

Dawn grinned. "I'll let Logan do that."

I regretted my decision the moment Dawn and I walked into Stoneybrook General Hospital.

A man was moaning in the waiting room. Next to him, a nurse was practically shouting in his ear, "Mr. Jones, did you take your medication today?"

Another nurse was taking the temperature of a little girl whose cheeks were all puffed up.

By the time Dawn and I arrived, the rest of the class was gathered by the reception desk. Shelley was deep in conversation with a familiar woman in a white coat.

"Hi, Dr. Johanssen!" Dawn and I said at the same time.

Dr. Johanssen happens to be one of our clients, the mom of an eight-year-old girl named Charlotte. Boy, was it a relief to see her smiling face in a place like this.

"Welcome, girls!" Dr. Johanssen said. "Dawn, it's so nice to see you again."

As she and Dawn chatted, I walked over to Logan, who was standing near the back of the crowd. He put his arm around me and whispered, "Sorry for being so crabby."

That made me feel a little better. But not much.

"Now, Dr. Johanssen is going to take us on a brief tour," Shelley announced, "after which we'll go back to class and discuss what we saw."

We followed Dr. Johanssen out of the waiting room and into a corridor. The walls were bright white, lined with half-open doors on both sides.

The quiet of the waiting room instantly gave way to shouting and electronic beeping.

"Dr. Bauman, room four . . . fibrillation STAT . . . MRI results . . . head trauma in five . . . STAT . . . reduce the intercranial pressure on Urgent One . . . increase the adrenaline . . . CAT scan . . . dog scan . . . dancing the can can . . ."

Well, something like that. The sounds were blending together, making no sense. It was creepy. I imagined myself as an emergency patient. I'd be petrified. The last thing I'd want to hear is all that loud medical chatter. Maybe some soft music instead.

"Stoneybrook General may be small in size," Dr. Johanssen was explaining, "but we are as up-to-date as any major urban teaching hospital in the Northeast."

That was reassuring, I guess.

I kept peeking into the rooms, half expecting to spot some horrible, bloody mess. But all I saw were calm, bored-looking people in blue robes.

"Mary Anne?" Logan said gently as we stopped at the end of the hallway.

I looked up at him. His eyes were soft and questioning. He had that *I need to tell you something* look.

My heart jumped. He'd talked to his dad. They'd fought it out. Logan was staying. I just knew it. "Yes?" I asked.

"Would you stop squeezing my hand so tightly?"

"Oh. Sorry."

I let go. Shelley was lecturing us about concussions or something. A nurse pushed a teenage boy in a wheelchair past us. His ankle was bandaged up.

"Hi, Jason," Dr. Johanssen greeted him. "This is a summer first-aid course from the Stoneybrook Community Center."

He nodded toward us. "Yo, don't play with fireworks!" he called out, lifting his foot.

Ugh. That fluttery feeling in my stomach was coming back.

"When Jason first came here," Dr. Johanssen said, "we weren't sure we could save his foot . . ."

I didn't want to hear this. I grabbed Logan's hand again.

"Dr. Johanssen!" a voice called urgently from behind me.

I turned. A nurse was walking briskly down the hall, trailed by a woman in a summer dress and a tall man in a Hawaiian shirt. Slumped over the man's shoulder was a motionless little boy who looked about two or three years old. He was wearing a tank top, terrycloth shorts, and tiny blue jellies on his feet, which were dangling limply.

"Seizure!" the nurse shouted.

"Room Seven!" Dr. Johanssen snapped.

"Against the wall, please!" Shelley shouted.

We all backed away to let the nurse and the family pass. They rushed into a room across the hall, followed by Dr. Johanssen.

I don't believe I will ever forget the expression on the dad's face. It was like a scared child's, frozen with panic. His eyes were wide and glassy, glaring straight ahead as if they could bore a hole through anything in his way.

I choked on a gasp.

From where I was standing, I could see the nurse take the little boy from the dad. As she lay the boy on a white-sheeted bed, I caught a glimpse of his eyes. They were white. The eyeballs had rolled back.

I thought I was going to lose it.

Logan put his arm around my shoulder. I was sure Shelley would usher us away, but she didn't. Inside the room, no one seemed to notice we were there.

Dr. Johanssen was firing off instructions in a calm but firm voice. Instantly the parents were undressing the boy to his diapers, the nurse was taking the boy's temperature, and Dr. Johanssen was poking and prodding.

"Blood pressure's low, temperature's up," Dr. Johannsen announced. "He's dehydrated."

The nurse quickly began preparing an intravenous tube. Dr. Johanssen turned to the parents. "He'll be all right," she said. "That's the first thing you need to know. Now, would you tell me what happened?"

The mom's voice was hoarse and weak. "He's been running a fever since last night. He wasn't holding any food down, not even the Tylenol we tried to give him."

"We were having company today, and it was hot inside the house," the dad continued. "So I took him outside to let him rest on the hammock. He fell right asleep. Then . . ." He took a deep breath and choked back a sniffle. "Then he started to . . . to . . ."

"Convulse," Dr. Johanssen said gently.

The man nodded. "His body started flopping

around, his eyes rolled up. I just grabbed him and yelled for Susan, and we jumped into the car to come here."

"Has this happened before?" Dr. Johanssen asked.

Both parents said no.

"Any epilepsy in the family?"

No again.

Dr. Johanssen turned to the boy and felt his forehead. His left arm was hooked up to the IV now. He looked so small and helpless, lying there in only a little white plastic diaper.

I began sobbing quietly. Logan put his arm around me.

"His temperature is a hundred and five," Dr. Johanssen said gravely to the parents. "Under the age of five or so, a child's nervous system is immature. A sudden spike in temperature like this can throw the body into a condition we call febrile seizure. It's not unusual, and even though it's scary to see, it is not harmful. Usually all we do is keep the child safe and work to bring the body temperature down — lukewarm baths, acetaminophen suppositories in the case of a child who is spitting up, whatever it takes."

"You mean, this is normal?" the mom asked. "He's going to be all right?"

Dr. Johanssen smiled. "I believe so."

What a relief. I slumped against Logan. I

could see my friends all smiling and murmuring to one another. Even Shelley Golden had tears in her eyes.

"Just to be on the safe side, though," Dr. Johanssen said, "I want to rule out spinal meningitis. Which means I need to take a spinal tap."

Both parents' faces sank. "What does that involve?" the father asked.

"Well, after he's awake and alert," Dr. Johanssen replied, "we extract some fluid from the base of the spine. Now, the syringe has to be placed exactly, so I'll need you two to hold him . . ."

I felt my stomach rising up toward my mouth like a rubber band. "Let's go," I muttered to Logan.

Shelley already had the same idea. She was leading the class toward the waiting room.

I have never walked so fast in my life.

Wednesday

Now hear this! Now hear this! Yours truly, Kristy Thomas, had a febrile seizure at the age of three. Mom told me last night. And you see how brilliant and alert and wonderful I turned out? (No comments, please.)

I thought about teaching febrile seizure awareness to the Pike kids today, but Mal talked me out of it.

It would only scare them. Besides, they're all older than five, which means they're past the danger point.

Right. So we decided on another safety lesson. One that's useful to all ages. . . .

"I'm driving the hook and ladder truck!" Claire Pike shouted. "RRRRRRRRRRR . . ."

"I get to use the ax!" Nicky Pike yelled.

"I spray the hose!" Margo Pike called out.

"I'm the Dalmatian — rowf! Rowf!" Vanessa Pike barked.

Adam Pike burst out laughing. *"Dalmatian?"*

"Yes," Vanessa replied. "All firehouses have Dalmatians. Didn't you know that?"

I guess you know what Kristy's idea was.

I am very glad she didn't try to teach the kids about febrile seizures. Why traumatize them? I was still a basket case myself. I barely remember leaving the hospital. I know we all walked back to the Stoneybrook Community Center, and I know we finished the class, but I was in such a daze, I couldn't tell you what we learned.

Oh, in case you were wondering, the little boy was all right. Dawn called Dr. Johanssen on Tuesday night to check. He did not have spinal meningitis, and he left the emergency room with flowers, lollipops, a near-normal temperature, and two very relieved parents.

In the twenty-four hours or so afterward, I discovered that lots of people knew about febrile seizures. Kristy, Anna Stevenson, a niece of Sharon's, Jessi's cousin — all of them had had one.

Still, the thought of that boy haunted me. The visit had shaken me up. I was on the verge of quitting first-aid class.

Some tiger I was. More like a scaredy-cat.

Kristy, of course, had fully recovered by the time of her sitting job. In fact, she was bitten by the emergency-safety bug. With the Firefighters' Fair around the corner, she decided fire safety would be the theme of the day.

It was a good idea. Mallory has enough brothers and sisters to form a real fire department. Seven, to be exact. Claire is the youngest. She's five years old. In ascending order, Margo is seven, Nicky eight, Vanessa nine, and the triplets (Adam, Jordan, and Byron) ten.

"WEEE-OOOO, WEEE-OOOO, WEEE-OO!" Byron was wailing.

"We have a four-alarm fire at One Thirty-four Slate Street!" Jordan announced, cupping his hand around his mouth like a megaphone. "The place is burning up!"

Claire looked horrified. "Hey, that's our house!"

"All the kids have survived except the littlest one!" Jordan continued. "She's melting like the Wicked Witch of the West — "

"Make him stop!" Claire pleaded.

"Jordannnn," Mallory scolded.

"Okay, guys, what if your house *is* burning?" Kristy asked. "What do you do?"

"Say, '*AHHHHHHH!*' " Claire screamed.

"Call nine-one-one," Nicky suggested.

"Turn on the faucet all the way and stick your finger in it!" Byron blurted out. "You can make the water shoot out, right at the fire!"

"Roast hamburgers," Adam volunteered.

"No, s'mores!" Vanessa exclaimed.

"Nicky's on the right track," Mallory said. "But what if you can't get to a phone?"

"Open the window and yell for a neighbor," Margo answered.

"Like this: '*AHHHHHHH!*' " Claire demonstrated.

"Ow, my eardrums!" Jordan moaned.

"Okay, you're in your room, your door is closed, and you smell smoke," Kristy continued. "Now what?"

"Push the door open and run away, of course!" Nicky said.

Kristy shook her head. "But you might run right into the fire. So first you feel the door and the doorknob."

"If it's hot, forget it!" Adam piped up. "Out the window you go."

"Well, you do keep the door closed, because that keeps the smoke out temporarily," Kristy said. "But you don't jump, Adam. Not until you've attracted your neighbors' attention and someone has called the fire department. They can lower you safely to the ground with ladders."

"What if your door isn't hot?" Mallory asked.

"Meep-meep!" Vanessa said, imitating the Road Runner and darting away.

"Not so fast," Kristy called out. "Do you know what causes the most harm in a fire?"

"Burning flames that melt your flesh and make your eyes dribble out!" Adam said.

"Ewwww," Margo groaned.

"Dribble out?" Claire's bottom lip was quivering.

Mallory put an arm around her little sister. "Don't listen to him. *Smoke* is what hurts people the most. If you breathe too much of it, it can burn your lungs."

"But what does hot air do?" Kristy asked.

Seven blank stares.

"Make popcorn?" Nicky finally guessed.

Kristy shook her head. "It rises. Which means the air will be cooler and clearer near the floor. So if you do see smoke, you do three things — stop, drop, and roll. *Stop* the moment you see it, *drop* to the floor, and *roll* as far as you can. Like this."

Kristy demonstrated (very dramatically, I'm sure). Immediately the kids tried to imitate her. Margo flopped onto the grass. Vanessa rolled over her, giggling. Nicky sprawled on his back and Claire sat on him. The triplets rolled all the way to the next-door neighbors' fence.

"I won!" Jordan proclaimed, jumping to his feet.

"It wasn't a race!" Byron protested.

"I'll race you!" Nicky challenged.

The kids scurried into a rough line, giggling and jostling each other.

"Uh, guys . . ." Mallory called out.

Kristy reached into her backpack for her referee's whistle. (Yes, she actually brings one to most of her jobs. It works wonders when she needs to attract the attention of unruly kids.)

"Okay, everyone lined up?" Kristy asked in her best gym-teacher voice.

"Yeeeeaaaahh!" the kids replied.

"Kristy, what are you doing?" Mallory asked.

"If you can't beat 'em . . ." Kristy said with a grin. She raised the whistle to her lips and shouted, "Stop . . . drop . . . *roll!"*

Phweeeeeet!

"Remember your spending limit," Mrs. Bruno said, pulling her car to a stop in front of Bellair's.

"Okay, Mom," Logan replied, as he and I climbed out.

"And let Mary Anne help you," Mrs. Bruno continued. "She has a good sense of style."

"Uh-huh," Logan said.

"Afterward, use the credit card to take yourselves out for a nice lunch. Call me when you need a ride back."

"Yup."

"Thanks, Mrs. Bruno," I said. "That's really nice of you."

Logan and I said good-bye to his mom and walked toward Bellair's front doors. The air was warm, but a cool breeze was blowing.

It would have been a perfect day if it weren't for our mission. We were going to shop for Logan's boot-camp clothes.

Neither of us was looking forward to that.

Logan seemed to be in his own world. I smiled at him once or twice, but he didn't seem to notice.

"Are you angry about something?" I finally asked.

"I hate shopping," Logan murmured.

"Oh. I thought maybe you'd had a fight with your mom or dad."

"Why would I do that?"

"Well, you know, about the summer, about prep school . . ."

"Nahh, we don't talk about that stuff anymore."

"So I guess that's it? You're going? You're not even trying?"

Logan glared at me. "Why should I? Do you *want* me to fight with them?"

"I didn't say that, Logan. I'm just surprised you gave up."

"I didn't give up! I just — " Logan stopped himself. He looked straight ahead and walked in stony silence.

I didn't say a thing. I was afraid I'd just make things worse. Or start crying. Or both.

"You know," Logan finally said with a sigh, "in football practice, you learn to tackle by running into these huge padded cylinders. It's supposed to make you more aggressive. But you can never *actually* tackle them. They're balanced on this sturdy metal frame. You're like an animal doing the same thing over and over for no reason. Well, that's what arguing with my dad is like. I just don't want to keep doing it."

I nodded. "So because of that, you're just going to throw away years of your life in a place you don't want to be in."

"No! I mean, yes. I mean, why do you have to put it that way?"

"Because it's true, Logan. Isn't it?"

Logan fell silent.

"Remember when your teammates were teasing you about being in the BSC?" I pressed on. "You tried to ignore them. You figured they'd go away. But they just made you more and more miserable. Finally you stood up to them, and it worked. They backed down."

"My parents aren't my teammates, Mary Anne."

"I know! But the point is, if you don't fight back for something you want, you lose."

Logan laughed. "I never thought I'd hear you say something like that."

"They're *your* words, Logan," I grumbled. "You told them to me. Maybe you should try to live by them."

I could not believe I had said that. It had just slipped out of my mouth.

I hate being crabby. I hate arguing. But boy,

was I angry. And not only at Logan. Mostly I was angry at Mr. Bruno. How could he be so insensitive? Didn't he see how awful his son was feeling?

I could feel tears rushing into my eyes. I tried to choke them back. I sounded like a vacuum cleaner that had just sucked up a stuffed animal.

"Don't worry," Logan said, putting his arm around me.

That did it. My cheeks became water slides. "I'll just miss you, that's all," I said.

"Look, maybe it won't work out. Maybe Dad'll be happy if I just go to this camp. Maybe he'll miss me so much, he'll give up the idea of prep school."

Logan was smiling. I knew he meant that last remark as a joke.

Somehow, though, I did not find it funny.

I did not want to be in Bellair's. The fresh-cut flowers, the smell of colognes, the lights, the bright displays — they were all disturbing my gloom.

Logan fished a wrinkled-up piece of legal paper out of his pants pocket. "Mom wrote out this list of stuff."

I took the paper. Maybe if I shifted into shopping mode, I would forget my problems. Smoothing the list out, I began reading:

" 'Short-sleeve button-down shirt, tank top, utility shorts, bug spray, sunglasses, white socks . . .' "

We went straight to the young men's section. The first thing I saw was a display of gorgeous plaid shirts.

"How about madras?" I asked.

"I'm not supposed to bring a bed to camp," Logan said.

"*Madras,* not *mattress*! It's a kind of plaid design on cotton." I gestured toward the shirts.

"Nice." Logan sounded about as excited as if I'd discovered a crate full of cauliflower.

I began rummaging through the piles. "Maybe a nice blue-green pattern . . ."

I found a pretty shirt and turned around. Logan was gone.

"Logan?" I called out. "Logan?"

I looked around the nearest corner into the cross aisle. No Logan.

The smell of chocolate wafted by me on a gust of air-conditioning. I glanced toward the source of the smell, to my left. A sign pointed around a corner, saying UNCLE CHIP'S COOKIE KITCHEN.

I followed. Logan was standing with a small crowd of people around a young woman carrying a tray of chocolate-chip cookie samples.

"Hi, foo fum — " Logan swallowed a mouthful of cookie and tried again: "Try some! They're free."

The woman turned politely toward me. "Thank you," I said, taking a small sample. "Uh, Logan . . ."

Logan grabbed another fistful. "I know, I know. We're supposed to shop."

As we headed back to the men's department, Logan peered at the list. " 'Utility knife'?"

" *'Shorts,'* " I corrected him. "Utility shorts. What are they?"

Logan shrugged. "I don't know."

I spotted a man in a Bellair's uniform who was tidying a stack of pants. "Excuse me," I asked. "What are utility shorts?"

"You may want to try junior misses on the second floor," the man answered.

"No, it's for him — "

I turned toward Logan. Gone again.

"Excuse me."

Groan. The guard must have thought I'd lost my mind.

This time I found Logan looking at the Swiss Army knives.

"These are cool," he said.

"Not on the list," I reminded him.

"Right. Sorry."

Before we were finished, we'd looked at dirt bikes, video games, football equipment, and paperback books. Plus we visited Stacey's mom, who works in the Bellair's buying department. And for good measure, we made a couple more stops at the kitchen of Uncle Chip.

We trudged out of the store, carrying two huge Bellair's bags. I was exhausted.

I was also looking forward to that lunch Mrs. Bruno had offered us.

"Rosebud Cafe?" Logan asked.

"As fast as we can," I said.

A couple of other restaurants are closer to Bellair's, but the Rosebud is a special place. Logan works there as a busboy, and all the restaurant personnel are always friendly to us.

We were sweaty and hot by the time we arrived, but the air-conditioning was on full blast, and it felt wonderful. The place was almost empty, and a great tune was playing on the jukebox.

Terry Dutton, one of the other busboys, was clearing our favorite table by the window. He broke into a grin when he saw us. "Heyyyy, guys, in for a farewell lunch?"

Farewell lunch. The words hit me like a hammer.

"Uh, it's not farewell, Terry," Logan said, slipping into a seat.

"You mean, you talked your old man out of it?" Terry asked.

Carlos Nuñez, one of the waiters, was rushing by on the way to the kitchen. "You're not leaving after all?"

"Well, no," Logan said. "I mean, it's still only June — "

"Hey, Mr. Fee!" Carlos called out. "Bruno's staying in town!"

"Wait!" Logan protested, "I didn't say that — "

But Carlos was barging into the kitchen. And Mr. Fee, the owner of the Rosebud, was approaching us with a big grin. "We-e-ell, that's good news!" he said. "I gave away most of your hours, but I'm sure we can — "

"Uh, sorry, Mr. Fee, but I *am* going away," Logan blurted out. "Just not for a few weeks, that's all."

Mr. Fee looked at him curiously. "Oh. Well, if you should change your mind . . ." His voice trailed off as he walked away.

Terry wiped off the glass tabletop and handed us two menus. "A few weeks, huh? Bummer."

My feelings exactly.

Maybe this *was* a farewell lunch.

"Do you know what you want?" Logan asked.

"Yeah, I want you to talk to your dad!"

No, I didn't say those words. I just thought them. As hard as I could. In Logan's direction.

I'm surprised they didn't burn a hole through the menu.

"I cannot wait to be a victim!" Dawn exclaimed. "I was *born* to be a victim."

"Dawn, you're sick," said Claudia.

"Seriously," Dawn continued. "I can scream great. It's an art, you know. A friend of my stepmother's in L.A. screams professionally. The TV and movie studios hire her for disaster scenes."

"What a great way to make a living," Stacey said.

"Do you have to go to college for that?" Logan asked.

"Totally, totally sick," Claudia remarked.

It was Saturday, and we were heading for Stoneybrook Boulevard, where the First Annual Stoneybrook Safety Weekend festivities were about to begin. The organizers had been working really hard at it. Shelley had even postponed Friday's class to Tuesday.

Dawn, as you can tell, was pretty thrilled

about the Disaster Drill. I was not. Pretending to be a victim was about the last thing I wanted to do.

I'd had enough of being the real thing.

"Don't you think this is a little weird?" I asked. "A make-believe accident where a bunch of kids pretend to be injured?"

"It's a demonstration," Stacey said. "I mean, if you saw a video on first aid, and someone was setting a broken bone or doing mouth-to-mouth, you'd be watching actors, right? So this is just like that, only live."

"I shall use my ahhhcting skills," Jessi said in a dramatic voice. "Gadzooks, methinks my leg bone breaketh!"

"Give her the hook!" Claudia shouted.

"Well, I'm not going to do it," Mallory declared. "I'll just watch."

"Me, neither," Stacey agreed. "A Disaster Drill? It reminds me of the dentist."

"Hey, where's your team spirit?" Claudia asked. "Shelley needs us. What's the big deal? You lie on the street, cry out for help — "

"Lovely," Stacey said. "Lying in all those germs in the hot sun and ruining my new summer outfit?"

"I'll do just about anything," Logan said, "but I refuse to be beheaded."

I poked him in the ribs.

We jabbered away until we reached Stoneybrook Boulevard. There, three entire blocks had been cordoned off.

Police officers were erecting barricades along the curbs. Emergency medical technicians in white uniforms scurried around, shouting instructions through bullhorns. A few old cars were lined up, single file, at the end of the second block. One by one, the drivers moved forward according to the shouted directions. The first one drove slowly up a curb and stopped just short of a light pole.

"Cool," Jessi said. "They're choreographing an accident."

A small crowd had begun to form. I spotted Kristy and her brothers among them, and we joined them.

"Hi," I said. "Where's Abby?"

"She didn't want to come," Kristy said, "when she found out it was going to be a car accident."

I felt a knot in my stomach. Poor Abby. The memories of her dad's crash were still so strong.

I was distracted by the sight of Shelley, running toward us in the middle of the commotion, holding a clipboard. "Oh, good, our first victims are here early!"

"Uh, Shelley?" Stacey spoke up. "We don't all have to do this, do we?"

"Of course not," Shelley replied. "We just need, oh, five or six victims so that the EMTs can demonstrate their techniques. Everything will be done slowly. Someone will be narrating each step. You'll be actors. We'll even have a little makeup and fake blood to spice things up a bit."

Gulp. Fake blood? I did not like the sound of this. Not at all.

Shelley scanned a sheet of paper on her clipboard. "Let's see . . . I'll need a head-trauma victim, a heavy bleeder, a broken leg, a fainter, two victims in the car, front and backseats — "

"And a paaaartridge in a peaaaar treeee!"

The singing voice of Alan Gray was unmistakable. Like fingernails scratching a blackboard.

"Maybe *Alan* can be beheaded," Logan said.

Alan shrugged. "Cool."

"It wouldn't change anything," Kristy muttered.

Shelley looked at her watch. "Okay, we have some time. It's eleven forty-five, and the predisaster festivities start at noon. The various departments are setting up booths. The police station is having an open house. The EMTs are giving demonstrations of their equipment. And some of the local stores have provided refreshments at the end of the second block. The Disaster Drill itself won't begin until one o'clock. So let me assign volunteers first, and then you can browse around."

"Does the head-trauma victim scream?" Dawn asked.

"Maybe not," Shelley replied. "The broken leg might."

"Sign me up," Dawn said.

Shelley chuckled. "So eager. I like that. Now, how about the heavy bleeder?"

"How about a vampire to clean it up, nyah-hah-hah!" Alan said.

"Ah, Alan!" Shelley said. "The bleeder is a perfect role for you! Very dramatic."

Alan turned green. "I was kidding! I'm not going to lie in a pool of blood. Yuck!"

"Any other volunteers?" Shelley asked.

Silence.

Dawn gave an exasperated sigh. "Come on, Mary Anne," she muttered.

"Ohhhh, no," I said. "Uh-uh. Nope."

"It's only make-believe," Dawn whispered.

"I know that! But — "

"It's kind of the starring role," Claudia said. "People will have tears in their eyes."

"Then why don't *you* do it?" I asked.

"I want to be the fainter," Claudia replied.

"Nobody?" Shelley asked, glancing my way.

I tried to shrink back into the crowd.

"Mary Anne will do it!" Dawn blurted out. "Right?"

I was flabbergasted. "Me? I — "

"Great!" Shelley said, scribbling on the pad. "How about the passengers?"

"I — I — " I sputtered.

"Only one job per person, Mary Anne," Shelley reprimanded me.

"I'll be a passenger!" Kristy called out.

"Me, too!" Alan volunteered.

"I changed my mind!" Kristy shot back.

I stood there, totally ignored, my jaw practically scraping the ground.

Heavy bleeder? No way. At that point, I was better suited for shock victim.

I was in a daze. I couldn't believe that Dawn — Dawn Schafer, my stepsister, who was supposed to love me — had betrayed me like this. Yes, I told that to her (in much nicer words). Her reaction? "You'll be a star, Mary Anne!"

I tried to talk to Logan about it, too. He kept saying it was no big deal.

It's no big deal. I kept repeating that to myself. Everybody was saying it. I needed to be brave. I needed to get over my fears. This wasn't real blood. It wasn't a real accident.

I was a nervous wreck. During the "predisaster festivities" I just wandered among the booths. Aimlessly. I'm sure I said hi to a few people, but I don't recall the details.

Finally I decided I could not do it. I elbowed my way through the crowd toward Shelley. As I approached, she looked at her watch.

"Shelley — " I began.

"Thanks for reminding me, Mary Anne!" Shelley said excitedly. "Ben, here's our bleeder! Her name is Mary Anne. Would you prepare her, please?"

A young guy in an emergency-medical-technician uniform bounded over to me with a big smile. He was carrying an apron and a bucket of thick red liquid. "You're going to love this," he said.

Ben brought me out to the street. We stopped near a car that had been parked diagonally across the road, as if it had just skidded to a stop.

"This is water, corn starch, and food coloring," he said. "This apron will wrap around you, but you don't really need it. The stuff'll come out easily in the wash. We scrubbed the pavement this morning, too."

"Uh-huh," I squeaked.

He had this eager, *boy-isn't-this-fun?* look on his face as he dumped the contents of the bucket onto the street.

It did look like blood. My stomach knotted right up.

"I have to . . . lie in this?"

He nodded. "Go ahead. I'll put some on you, too, if you want. Make it look realistic."

Be brave, Mary Anne.

I gritted my teeth, put on the apron, and lay down. The liquid felt warm and icky. I thought I was going to lose my breakfast. "Uh, don't pour any more," I said.

"Okay," Ben said, turning away. "Good luck."

I could see the crowd collecting behind the police barricades. Alan and Kristy were being led to one of the cars. Claudia was sitting on the road, waiting for her signal to faint. Logan, who was going to be the head-trauma victim, was deep in conversation with a nurse.

As Dawn walked past me with an EMT, she was beaming. "Looks great!" she exclaimed.

Me? I felt like a fool. People were staring. Jamie Newton, a four-year-old BSC charge, saw me and burst into tears.

"Ladies and gentlemen," Shelley announced, "the Stoneybrook emergency services personnel present a mock Disaster Drill, featuring the students of my first-aid class!"

A smattering of applause rang out.

The demonstration began with Claudia the fainter. They had to determine how badly hurt she was. Then they had to rouse her and check her vital signs.

My attention started to fly away. I was hot. The fake blood was starting to dry up. And it smelled.

I thought they'd never get to me. When they did, one of the EMT workers who handled me was shaking. She applied a tourniquet way too tightly. She was dripping sweat onto my face. And she almost dropped me off the stretcher.

Now people were laughing — laughing! I was slowly slipping from humiliation to pure fury.

When they finally loaded me into the back of an ambulance, a huge cheer went up.

I didn't care one bit.

The EMTs congratulated me, and I politely thanked them. Inside, though, I was steaming. I took off my apron and let it drop to the floor. As I climbed out of the ambulance, I felt grimy, dirty, and sticky. Dawn was waiting for me, smiling brightly.

"You see?" she said. "Wasn't that fun?"

I couldn't even look her in the eye. "As a matter of fact," I said, storming away, "it was one of the worst days of my life."

CHAPTER 11

Whack!

I slammed my bedroom door. I didn't care if I broke the doorjamb.

I was mad.

Not to mention hideous. In front of my bedroom mirror, for the first time all day, I could see what I looked like.

My hair was tangled. My left cheek had a smudge mark from the street. My shirt collar was ripped. And my forearms were caked with dried fake blood.

I have never felt so dirty and disgusting in my life.

This was what the people in the crowd had seen?

No wonder they were laughing at me.

Why did I let myself do it?

You didn't, I reminded myself. If Dawn hadn't volunteered me, I would have been a nice, clean, normal spectator.

Tigger, who had been curled up on my bed, was now on all fours, staring at me.

Some people say animals do not have facial expressions. Well, they are so wrong. You should have been Tigger's face. He looked horrified.

"I know, Tiggy, it's awful," I said. "But it's fake. And it's all Dawn's fault."

Tigger curled around my ankles and began licking a few flecks of the red stuff off my socks.

I had to change clothes and wash up before Sharon and Dad came home. I grabbed a bathrobe out of my closet.

Knock-knock-knock!

"Mary Anne, are you okay?" came Dawn's voice from the other side of the door.

I swung the door open and faced her. "Does this look okay?"

Dawn smiled. "Yuck. Well, you're not the only one. One of the medics spilled orange soda all over Claudia in the ambulance."

"Excuse me, I have to take a shower," I said, shutting the door.

I am never, *ever* rude like that. But I could not help it. In my state, I was not responsible for my actions.

I changed into my bathrobe, grabbed my filthy clothes, and barged out the door. I didn't think Dawn would still be there, and I nearly ran into her.

She jumped back, and I went straight to the bathroom. I dumped my clothes in the hamper and took a long shower.

Dawn was sitting on my bed when I returned to my room.

"I need to change," I announced. "Would you leave, please?"

"Mary Anne, what's wrong?" Dawn asked. "You're never like this."

"Well, I've never spent a hot afternoon lying in the street in a pool of fake blood, with hundreds of people staring at me."

"*That's* what's bothering you?" Dawn said. "Then why did you volunteer?"

"I didn't! *You* volunteered me! Now, may I have some privacy, please?"

Dawn gave me a curious look. "Mary Anne, I'm your *sister*."

"Some sister you were, Dawn, pushing me into something I didn't want to do."

Dawn headed for the door, shaking her head. "Some things never change."

"Wait!" I called out. "What do you mean by that?"

"Mary Anne," Dawn said, turning around, "if you want something, you need to speak up. And if you don't, it's not always someone else's fault!"

With that, she closed the door and clomped downstairs.

I wanted to throw something. But I kept the feeling inside. I calmly got dressed. I brushed my hair. I gave Tigger a reassuring hug.

And then I burst into tears.

I was so tired of arguing. The summer had started out so well. And now it was turning into . . . well, a disaster.

It could not continue this way.

Taking a deep breath, I composed myself. I walked downstairs and found Dawn in the family room, sitting cross-legged on the floor. Her eyes were closed.

"Dawn?" I said.

She didn't answer for a moment. Then her eyes popped open. "I was trying to meditate."

"You know how to do that?"

"No. Do you? I think you're supposed to sit still and say 'Ommm' to yourself."

I couldn't help smiling. "Ommm?"

"I don't know," Dawn said with a shrug. "I just thought it might help make me feel better."

I wanted to laugh, but I didn't. Dawn might take it the wrong way.

Instead, I sat down quietly next to her. "Dawn, I'm sorry I yelled at you."

"That's all right. You have a lot on your mind."

"At Safety Day, I tried to tell you I didn't want to participate. I guess I just should have spoken up more."

"No, I should have listened more."

"No, it was noisy and confusing. I needed to be more forceful."

"You're wrong, Mary Anne. I was overexcited."

We both fell silent.

"Ommmmmm," Dawn said.

I cracked up. So did Dawn.

"See?" Dawn said. "Meditating does help. Even if you don't know how to do it."

I leaned back against the couch. "You're right. I haven't felt so good all week."

"This Logan thing has really been bothering you, huh?"

"Yeah. If you weren't here, Dawn, this would be my all-time worst summer. I feel so helpless."

Dawn nodded. "It's not as if *you* can go argue with the Brunos."

"Exactly. That's horrible thing number one. Horrible thing number two is first-aid class. *Everything* grosses me out. Even the pictures on the wall. I thought the class would help me. I thought I'd become braver. But I haven't. If an emergency happened, forget it. I'd be the last person in the world you'd want to have around."

Dawn sat up and looked at me quizzically. "That's not true, Mary Anne. You'd be the *first* person."

"Dawn, you don't have to try to make me feel better — "

"It's true, Mary Anne! Remember when you were baby-sitting for Jenny Prezzioso and she ran that super-high fever?"

"Do I ever," I replied. "A hundred and four."

"*She* didn't have a febrile seizure," Dawn said. "Why? Because you called the doctor. You arranged for an ambulance. You weren't scared one bit."

"I couldn't be. It was an emergency."

"That's my point. Don't sell yourself short, Mary Anne. When you need to act, you do."

"But at the airport — "

"You were just scared because you didn't know what to do. You didn't have the training. That's what the class is for. Guaranteed, if we were in a restaurant now, and I had something stuck in my throat, you'd be the first to maneuver my Heimlich."

"What's a Heimlich, anyway?" I asked.

"I think it's near the pancreas or something. I don't know."

The familiar noise of Dad's car filtered in through the window. We stood up, and Dawn opened the front door.

Dad and Sharon were pulling grocery bags out of the trunk. "Grilled tofu with scallions for dinner!" Sharon called out.

"Yummm!" Dawn exclaimed, running outside to help.

"Hamburgers for the carnivores!" Dad announced.

Suddenly I was starving. I still felt like a coward, but at least I wasn't angry anymore.

And my Heimlich was grumbling like crazy.

Sunday

Hip! Hip! Hurry! Today was the Firefitters' Fare! I got to take the Newtan kids, becuase there mom and dad had to visit a sick rellative.

Has anyone ever thot of rating the Fare? If they did, it shoud probably get a PG....

Claudia, as you can see, is not exactly a champion speller. Honestly, I'd never thought of the Firefighters' Fair as being PG, but I guess I'd never had an experience quite like Claudia's.

The fair is held every year in Stoneybrook's Old Fairgrounds, on the water. As you watch the events, you eat hot dogs and cotton candy and enjoy the sunset over Long Island Sound. After dark, fireworks begin.

Wholesome. Fun. Kid-friendly. Right?

Well, that's what Claudia was thinking when she walked over to the Newtons' house.

Mr. and Mrs. Newton greeted Claudia with weary, strained smiles at the front door.

"Hi, Claudia," Mrs. Newton said. "We're not quite ready to drive you all to the fair. Jamie has been a little reluctant."

"I'm not going!" Jamie's muffled, high-pitched voice rang out.

Claudia noticed that the sofa cushions looked much higher than usual. She pulled one up. "Peek-a-boo!"

Jamie curled up tightly. "Leave me alone!"

"He was a little rattled by the disaster demonstration yesterday," Mr. Newton explained.

"Look at Claudia, Jamie," Mrs. Newton pleaded. "She's fine."

Jamie peeked over his shoulder, then curled up again. "Yeah, but Mary Anne's *dead!*" he said.

Huh?

"Mary Anne's fine, too, Jamie," Claudia said, sitting next to him.

"No, she bleeded to death," Jamie insisted. "I saw her."

"That was make-believe, Jamie," Claudia said gently. "It wasn't real blood. Mary Anne will be at the Firefighters' Fair. You'll see."

"I'm not going!" Jamie shouted.

"Jamie, do as Claudia says," Mr. Newton called out.

Looking at her watch, Mrs. Newton said, "We still need to finish getting ready. Lucy's napping. I think they'd both enjoy the fair, but I'll leave it to your judgment, Claudia. We'd be happy to drop you off."

"NO! NO! NO! NO!" Jamie wailed.

As the Newtons slipped upstairs, Claudia leaned back into the couch cushions and sighed. "Jamie, you can be the boss. We don't have to go to the Firefighters' Fair if you don't want to."

Jamie sat up. "We don't?"

Claudia shook her head. "We can stay home and miss all the cotton candy and hot dogs and ice cream — "

"Ice cream?"

"Tons of it."

Jamie looked confused. "But ice cream melts."

"Not if it's in a freezer, Jamie — "

"But the fire will burn up the freezer. And then it will burn the people and kill everybody!"

Claudia put a comforting arm around him. "Look, I've been going to every Firefighters' Fair since I was a little girl. They do have a small fire. But it's just so the firefighters can show how the big fire engines work. Everyone watches it from a distance."

"Hook and ladder or pumper?"

"Uh, both, I think."

Jamie thought about that for awhile. "Well . . . I'm the boss, and I say, let's go have some cotton candy and then come home."

"Yes, sir!" Claudia saluted him. "Request permission to play Chutes and Ladders until baby sister wakes up, sir!"

"Yippeee!"

Jamie fetched the game from his toy cupboard. By the time Lucy woke up, he had won one game and was well on his way to a second.

Finally Mr. and Mrs. Newton were ready to leave. Jamie didn't protest a bit. In fact, he ran outside to the car.

Mrs. Newton was flabbergasted. "Claudia, you're a miracle worker," she said.

Claudia felt pretty good on the ride to the fair. Lucy was gurgling away in her car seat, and Jamie gradually fell asleep, nuzzled against Claudia's shoulder. (All the arguing must have worn him out.)

Traffic was thick near the Old Fairgrounds. Mr. Newton pulled to a stop about two blocks away. Then he and his wife took a collapsible double stroller out of the trunk and helped Claudia load the kids into it. As the Newtons climbed back in the car and waved good-bye, Claudia wheeled Lucy and Jamie toward the fair. Jamie was still fast asleep.

RRRRRRRRRR! HONK! HONK! blasted a fire engine as it roared past them.

"Eeeeeeee!" yelled Lucy gleefully.

"AAAAAAAAUUGGHH!" screamed Jamie.

Claudia stopped to watch. "Cool, huh?"

But Jamie was cringing in the stroller, his hands over his ears. *"Make them sto-o-o-op!"*

Oops. Time to move on.

The sidewalk was full of families now, and Claudia followed the flow around the old Stoneybrook town hall.

She was hit with a blast of salt air mixed with the smell of hot dogs and popcorn. At the edge of the Old Fairgrounds, a small Ferris wheel spun slowly atop a trailer. Next to it was a big, orange, rectangular moonwalk that bounced with the kids who were inside it. A clown in a firefighter's uniform was walking around on stilts, waving to the newcomers.

Claudia unhooked Jamie. He ran straight to the cotton candy.

Kristy, Logan, and I were standing nearby. We were being scolded by Dawn for eating "processed animal entrails and spun pancreas poison." (Translation: hot dogs and cotton candy.)

"Hi!" Claudia called out.

"Eeeee!" Lucy squealed happily.

Logan punched his fist into the air. "Yyyess! Someone else for Dawn to dump on."

"I wasn't *dumping,*" Dawn retorted. "I'm trying to help you — "

"Claudiaaaaaa, may I pleeeeeease have some cotton candy?" Jamie called out, running toward us. He stopped short when he saw me. "You're *not* dead!"

Logan burst out laughing. "Not until she eats a little more pancreas poison."

Jamie stared at my cotton candy. "It has *poison?*"

"He's just kidding," Claudia said, poking Logan in the ribs.

Of course, Claudia went to all the vendors. Before long, she and Jamie were sitting on a bench, sharing a cardboard box full of fried food, cotton candy, ice cream, and these sugar-coated balls of fried dough called zeppoles.

(Don't worry, Dawn was far away from them by then.)

Jamie was in heaven. He stuffed his face. He went on the moonwalk and Ferris wheel. He ran to the fire engines, which were now lined up behind the bleachers that surrounded the big oval track in the center of the field. He climbed into the hook and ladder truck, helped by a firefighter. He blew the horn and sounded the siren.

As a reward, Claudia bought him (and herself) more snacks.

When it was time for the big show, Jamie hugged Claudia, sliming her vintage black bell-bottoms with grease and sugar. "I *looooove* the Firefighters' Fair!"

"You want to stay, huh, boss?" Claudia asked.

"All night!" Jamie replied.

Claudia was relieved. She'd been looking forward to the show.

Lucy seemed perfectly happy, too, as Claudia headed for the bleachers. They settled in among the rest of us BSC members. Behind us were Jeff, the Pike kids, and various parents.

The sun was setting to our left, coloring the clouds a vivid orange. Around the track, a team of clowns was riding in an old, broken-down jalopy with the words FIER TWUCK painted on the side. A tiny, two-story wooden house stood in the center of the track, only about fifteen feet high.

One of the clowns broke away from the jalopy. Giggling, he threw a smoke bomb into the house. As the smoke billowed from the window, the other clowns stopped the car and piled out, pulling a garden hose. Of course, the hose tangled all around them, making them trip and fall.

"They're silly!" Jamie exclaimed, laughing.

Then the house exploded.

It was so loud, even Claudia jumped. The smoke had turned to flames.

Jamie screamed. Lucy burst into tears. The clowns ran away. One of them fell to the ground in a mock faint.

"He's dead!" Jamie exclaimed.

RRRRRRRRRRRRR! sounded a siren from behind us.

Lucy nearly leaped out of Claudia's arms.

Into the track area rushed the entire Stoneybrook fire department — hook and ladder, pumper, fire chief, you name it. Out came the hoses blasting water. Out came the hoses blasting foam with a deafening *FOOOOOOSH!*

"WAAAAAHHHHH!" replied Jamie.

"EEEEEEEE!" replied Lucy.

"It's all part of the act!" Claudia said.

On the field, some EMT people were loading the "unconscious" clown onto a stretcher, but he kept flopping off onto the ground.

Forget it. Jamie was gone. Off the deep end.

"I WANNA GO HO-O-O-O-OME!"

Some of the people in front of us were turning to stare. "My dear," one woman said in a huff, "those babies are too young to bring to this."

Claudia bolted to her feet. "Uh . . . 'bye, guys," she said to us.

With Lucy in one arm, the folded-up double stroller in the other, and Jamie clutching her shirttail, Claudia made her way along the crowded bench. "Excuse me . . . excuse me . . ."

"Can I give you a ride back?" Mrs. Pike called out.

"Sure! Thanks!" Claudia replied as she climbed down to the ground and strapped both sobbing kids into the stroller.

Mrs. Pike walked with her toward the exit. By the time they reached it, the kids had quieted down. They were both looking toward the field where the little house now stood, charred and wet but intact.

"Cooool," Jamie said.

"Are you sure you want to leave?" Claudia asked.

CRRRRACKK!

The little house fell over in a heap.

"EEEEEEEEEEEEEE!" shrieked the duo of Newtons.

Claudia and Mrs. Pike hightailed it through the exit.

One of the first rules of BSC baby-sitting: Sometimes you win, and sometimes you don't.

"I *love* it!" Dawn took a deep breath and set her beach chair back a notch. "It feels just like California."

I smiled and breathed in the warm, sweet air. "Exactly," I agreed.

"Well, maybe not *exactly* exactly," Dawn said. "You have to ignore the trees and the houses. They're very East Coast. And the air smells different — you know, the vegetation and humidity or whatever. So maybe you have to close your eyes and breathe shallow. But otherwise, we could be in Palo City right now!"

I wasn't exactly thinking of Palo City. Hollywood was more like it.

Not only because of the weather. It was the location, too. We were lounging around the pool in the Kormans' backyard. The Kormans are clients of ours who live in a house that out-mansions Kristy's mansion. The backyard pool is humongous.

I hardly ever have the chance to baby-sit for the Kormans. They live in the same neighborhood as Kristy, Abby, and Shannon. But when Mrs. Korman called the BSC and said that both she and her neighbors, the Hsus, needed a sitter, Dawn jumped at the opportunity. She claimed she was suffering pool deprivation.

So that was how Dawn and I ended up lounging around, soaking up rays, on a lazy Monday morning.

As Dawn settled back, our four charges ran ecstatically around us. Bill Korman is nine. His sister, Melody, is seven, and so is Scott Hsu. Timmy Hsu is six. (Bill and Melody's baby brother, Skylar, was with the Kormans at a toddler birthday party.)

Don't worry. We weren't being totally lazy. Baby-sitting for kids around a pool is hard work. You have to pay extra-special attention.

As a matter of fact, Mr. and Mrs. Korman have a rule: no adult supervision, no pool. Luckily, their next-door neighbor, Mr. Sinclair, had agreed to watch over us from his yard. He's retired, but he used to be a lifeguard and is trained in life-saving techniques. (Plus, he is the nicest man.)

"It's a beauty, eh?" Mr. Sinclair said, plopping himself down on a wicker chair. He was wearing a porkpie hat and sunglasses, and his nose was covered with zinc oxide. As he opened a paperback book, he took a swig from a can of soda.

"Weeeeeeee!" Bill screamed, jumping into the shallow end of the pool.

"You really ought to try something lower in sugar and caffeine," Dawn called to Mr. Sinclair.

Now, I love my sister dearly, but sometimes — just sometimes — she can really embarrass me. *"Daaaaawn!"* I whispered.

"What's that?" Mr. Sinclair said.

"Sugar and caffeine dehydrate the body," Dawn replied.

Mr. Sinclair looked quizzically at his cola can. "Is that so?"

Splash! In went Scott.

"Yikes! It's cold!" he called out.

Now Scott and Bill were standing side by side, teeth chattering. Melody and Timmy were still on the ledge, looking doubtful.

"Come on in!" Bill urged them.

"Uh-uh," Melody said.

"Too cold," Timmy added.

"Babies!" taunted Scott. With a flick of the wrist, he sent water splashing over the side of the pool.

Melody and Timmy jumped away. Dawn

was hit in the face with a cold shower. "Oh!" she gasped. "It isn't heated?"

"Heyyyyyy, surf's up!" bellowed the voice of Linny Papadakis.

"Banzaaaiiiii!" called his sister Hannie.

The two of them were racing across the backyard, dressed in bathing suits. Linny is nine and Hannie's seven. My BSC safety antennae went up immediately.

"Whoa, wait a minute!" I said. "You can't go in there without Mrs. Korman's permission!"

"We always swim in the pool," Linny explained.

"Yes, but not when the Kormans are gone," I protested.

"It's all right," Mr. Sinclair called out. "I've got my eye on them."

Dawn laughed. "Don't be a pool party pooper, Mary Anne."

I was outnumbered. "Okay."

Linny and Hannie leaped into the pool. Mr. Sinclair was watching them carefully, still clutching his can of cola.

I sat back and tried to relax.

Soon Timmy and Melody were in the water, too. Bill ran inside and brought out some Super-soakers, and before I knew it, a water war had started.

The kids were shrieking and laughing. Dawn and I had to move our chairs to avoid being blasted. Mr. Sinclair had given up on his paperback and was chuckling at the chaos.

"I, Neptune the sea god, shall swim away from this terror!" Linny declared. Plunging headfirst under the water, he swam to the deep side of the pool and emerged near the diving board.

"I, Rocktune the pool god, shall follow you!" Bill bellowed.

Linny hooted with laughter. "No such thing!"

The two older boys were soon climbing out. The younger kids were still at war at the shallow end.

Rrrrrriiinnnnng! jangled a phone from inside Mr. Sinclair's house.

"Oops, be right back." Mr. Sinclair rose from his seat still holding his can of cola. "I think I'll switch to lemonade while I'm in there. Less caffeine. You girls want some?"

"No thanks," we replied.

As he walked inside, Dawn muttered, "It's probably from a mix. Do you know how much sugar is in those?"

She made a face, then settled back in her chair.

"We're going to get a Frisbee!" Bill called out. He and Linny darted into the Kormans' house through the back door.

The smaller kids didn't even notice. From

what I gathered, they were playing merpeople versus earth people, which basically meant splashing each other like crazy and saying, "Die, invaders!"

I was feeling a little nervous. Mr. Sinclair had disappeared into his house, which was partially hidden from view by a big maple tree. Dawn had an eye on the kids, but it was a very sleepy eye.

The sun was starting to beat down steadily. Beads of perspiration were rolling down my forehead. I could just feel myself starting to burn. I have extremely light skin, and I'd forgotten to bring a hat.

I opened up my backpack and rummaged around for my bottle of sunscreen.

"I am the great Strepgerm, god of the fast escape!" I heard Timmy announce. "And you shall never catch me!"

I kept fishing around in my pack: an extra bathing suit, a pair of sunglasses, a copy of *Wuthering Heights* (my absolute favorite book), breath mints . . . sunscreen.

I took it out and read the label — SPF 45. Perfect.

As I squeezed some onto my palm, I looked out over the pool.

The kids were still at war in the shallow end. Well, three of them were — Hannie, Melody, and Scott. Timmy had swum away.

I stood up. I peered at him. Then I dropped my sunscreen and bolted to my feet. Timmy was in the deep end of the pool. His arms were flailing, and his body was bobbing under the water.

Now the other kids saw him.

"What are you doing?" Scott shouted. *"You can't swim!"*

That feeling came over me again. That same queasy feeling I'd had in the airport cafeteria. In first-aid class. In the Disaster Drill.

"Hel — !" Timmy shouted, before the word was cut off by a mouthful of water.

Help.

Call for help.

The words shot through my brain.

I unlocked my jaw. *"DAWN!"* I blurted out. *"CALL NINE-ONE-ONE! TIMMY'S DROWNING!"*

Dawn shot to her feet. She threw off her sunglasses.

At that moment, Timmy went under and began to sink.

Dawn screamed something. I couldn't tell what.

I wasn't thinking at all. I was moving. Fast. Toward the pool.

Timmy was underwater. He wasn't going to wait for 911.

The tile floor gave way beneath me and I was dropping into the water, clothes and all. To my left, the kids were huddled against the side of the pool. I caught a glimpse of Dawn's blonde hair streaking across the yard toward the back door.

The water closed over me. I was vaguely aware of the cold. But I was more aware of the limp figure near the bottom of the pool. The hair waving like dark sea grass. The weak stream of bubbles that floated upward from Timmy's nose and mouth.

I pumped hard with my arms and legs. I felt weighted down and I remembered I hadn't taken off my shoes. Too late to worry about that.

I pushed harder. Timmy was looming closer. His eyes were open but he didn't seem to see me.

What was I supposed to do?

Under the armpit.

The words snapped through my mind. Shelley's words from first-aid class. That was all I could recall from her lecture on drowning. The rest was a jumble.

I reached with my left arm and grabbed Timmy around the back. Holding tight, I pumped upward with my right arm and both legs.

Timmy was heavier than I expected. I seemed to be moving in slow motion. I glanced up. The sky shone through the surface of the water, rippling lazily as if it had been turned to gelatin. I knew it was just over my head. Maybe two feet. Still, I'd never seen anything so distant. My lungs were bursting. I felt as if I had a tight chain around my chest.

When my face broke through the surface, air rushed into my mouth. I felt as if I were swallowing a freight train. I gasped so loudly that the noise startled me.

I lunged toward the edge of the pool. Grabbing onto the lip, I tried to lift Timmy over.

I heard the quick tapping of bare feet. Then

Linny and Bill were in front of me, pulling Timmy's arms. They hoisted him out of the pool.

His body was completely limp now. I climbed up behind him, clasped my fists together at the base of his ribcage, and pulled.

Nothing happened. Timmy just flopped like a doll.

"Is he . . . alive?"

I suddenly became aware of Scott, Hannie, and Melody kneeling by my side.

I think I answered "Yes" to Scott's question. I don't know for sure. All I knew was that Timmy was not breathing.

Quickly, gently, I lay Timmy on his back.

Call 911. CPR is difficult. If it's done wrong, it's potentially dangerous.

I shut out Shelley's words. I had to do *something*.

I lifted his chin and tilted back his forehead. His mouth opened slightly.

What were the instructions? What had Shelley said about CPR for children?

Look. That was step number one.

I glanced at his chest. It was not moving.

Listen.

I didn't hear any breathing at all.

Feel.

I moved my cheek close to Timmy's mouth. Nothing. Not a hint of a breeze.

Dawn was yelling something from the Kormans' house. Mr. Sinclair's voice boomed out from the other direction. The kids were screaming. Crying.

Two rescue breaths.

That was the next step. I pinched Timmy's nostrils so no air would escape. Then I took a deep breath, sealed my mouth over Timmy's and blew deeply . . . once . . . twice . . .

"Out of the way!" Mr. Sinclair was shouting.

I felt a hand on my shoulder. I was yanked backward.

"No!" I shouted.

Timmy's body suddenly jerked.

He rolled to his side, gagging. Water gushed out of his mouth and nostrils.

Mr. Sinclair was in front of me now, hunched over Timmy. I scrambled around to the other side.

Timmy was coughing — loud, choking coughs that were turning his face red.

Then he sat up and looked around, his eyes wide open and bloodshot. Tears cascaded down his cheeks. He was crying. Wailing helplessly at the top of his lungs.

It was the most beautiful sound I had ever heard. He *was* alive!

My own eyes were cloudy with tears and pool water. I started laughing and sobbing at the same time. Mr. Sinclair was helping Timmy to his feet. Scott threw his arms around his brother, weeping uncontrollably, as Mr. Sinclair guided Timmy to a chair.

The other kids were gathering around the brothers, all jabbering away, asking questions.

Dawn put her arm around my shoulder. She was crying just as hard as I was.

WEEEE-OOOOO-WEEEE-OOOOO-WEEEE-OOO!

The ambulance siren cut through the quiet street. Moments later, a man and a woman in white uniforms came sprinting into the backyard.

"What happened?" the woman asked, kneeling next to Timmy.

"This young man almost drowned," Mr. Sinclair explained. "He seems to have swallowed a lot of water, but he's all right now."

Both technicians tried to examine Timmy, but he was still screaming, his eyes wild with fear.

"Well, he sure seems strong," the man said. "But let's bring him to the hospital for observation. Looks like you acted quite fast, sir. Good thing you were here."

Mr. Sinclair shook his head. "It wasn't me, it was this young lady," he said, gesturing toward me. "She saved Timmy's life."

* * *

I kept thinking of that sentence all the way to the hospital.

I couldn't help it. Dawn must have repeated it about twenty times before Mr. Sinclair and I climbed into the ambulance with Timmy and Scott.

Timmy calmed down on the ride. He stared out the windows, looking frightened as I tried to reassure him. At the hospital, Scott, Mr. Sinclair, and I answered questions while a doctor examined Timmy.

The Hsus arrived soon after, explaining that Dawn had tracked them both down at work. By that time, Timmy was smiling and happy.

"I almost drowned!" he exclaimed. "But Mary Anne saved me!"

I could tell the Hsus had heard the story already. But they listened carefully, their eyes moist.

Timmy was released soon after, and the Hsus drove me home. They could not stop thanking me.

As I sat in the back of the car, watching Scott and Timmy chatter and laugh, the whole thing began sinking in. I looked at Timmy and said to myself, *If it weren't for me, he might not be here.*

I'd done what Sharon had done at the airport. I hadn't fainted. I hadn't sat around mulling things over.

I'd jumped into an emergency and fixed it.

Me, Mary Anne Spier.

Mary Anne the Town Crier. Mary Anne the Chicken.

When the Hsu car pulled up in front of my house, Dawn, Jeff, and Logan were waiting out front. They stood and applauded as I climbed out and walked toward them.

"I am so proud of you!" Logan exclaimed.

"I called Shelley," Dawn said. "She's going to make a big fuss over you in class."

"Oh, no!" I exclaimed.

Logan put his arm around me. "Tell us the whole story. Did you really lift Timmy over your head and swim only with your legs?"

"Whaaaat?" I said.

Dawn shrugged. "That's what Hannie told me."

We all sat in the living room. As I went over the story for Logan, Dawn disappeared into the kitchen. Jeff scurried after her. I tried to remember every detail. It all came flowing out, like a dream you suddenly remember after you've been awake for hours.

That was exactly how I felt. Awake. Wide awake.

Logan was hanging onto every word. When I finished, he let out a long, low whistle. "Whoa, I don't think I could ever be so calm in an emergency."

Another time I would have reassured him. Another time I would have thought he was crazy for even suggesting that I could be calm.

But I was seeing things differently now. Sure, I'd acted quickly when I thought Timmy was dying. It was an emergency. Emergencies bring out the best in people. Besides, I'd had a little first-aid training, so my confidence was up. But life is full of emergencies. Not just huge, life-and-death ones. Smaller ones, too. Ones we all have "training" for.

And whenever you face one, you have to make the same decision I did: jump in or stay back.

Up until now, I'd always thought of Logan as a jumper. But he was facing an emergency. A pretty big one, too. And his knees were locked.

"Logan, have you talked to your dad yet?" I asked.

Logan looked surprised. "What brought that up?"

"It's just been on my mind. And we haven't had much time alone lately." I smiled. "I guess I'm also feeling pretty brave after today."

Logan nodded. "I wish I felt the same way,

Mary Anne. I feel like a total coward compared to you."

Whoa. I never thought I'd hear *that*.

"Look," I said, "this whole thing is making your life miserable. You don't want to go to the camp. You don't want to go to prep school. And you have good reasons. Ones that any grown-up would understand. I know you think it's useless to talk to your dad — "

"That's not it," Logan murmured. "I know it's not *useless*."

"So what's wrong?"

Logan shrugged and looked away. "I just don't want to."

"Why? Are you scared?"

"No!" Logan shot back. "Well, maybe."

"What would happen if you sat down with him?" I asked. "Really told him how you felt, one-on-one?"

"He'd yell at me, I guess. He'd think I was a sissy or something."

"Because you stood up for yourself?"

"I wouldn't be doing the things *he* did when he was my age. All that stuff is important to him."

"You're not him, Logan! He must know that, deep inside."

"How do you know?"

"Look, my dad used to make me dress like a

little girl all the time. He treated me as if I would never grow up. He wasn't trying to be mean. He just wasn't seeing who *I* was. But you know what? For the longest time, I didn't tell him. I didn't want to offend him. So I just cried myself to sleep. When I finally did talk to him, he understood completely. He felt bad. And I realized I'd been *sooooo* stupid for waiting."

Logan looked at the floor for the longest time. When he finally spoke, his voice was almost a whisper.

"Would you be in the room when I do it? I mean, Dad really likes you. It couldn't hurt."

I couldn't help smiling.

Oh, well, I guess we all have our own ways of dealing with emergencies.

"It's a deal," I said.

"Okay, time's up," Shelley Golden announced. "Put your exams on the front desk on your way out, and have a fun — and safe — rest of the summer! I have thoroughly enjoyed this class!"

We all stood up and gave Shelley a big cheer. We'd only had four sessions, but I felt as if I'd been taking the class for a long, long time.

I sure had learned a lot. I'd found that out on Monday night when I'd studied for our final exam. And the test had not been easy, but I was pretty confident I'd done well.

"What did you get for number six?" Kristy whispered as I gathered up my stuff. "You know, the one about the pulmonary artery?"

"I left it blank," Alan Gray volunteered.

"Like the rest of your head," Kristy said.

"Ooooh, a direct hit, right between the eyes!" Irv remarked.

Alan was smiling as he brought his test to

the front desk. (Honestly, I believe he enjoys being insulted.)

"Oh, don't forget to take another piece of cake on the way out!" Shelley reminded us.

A half-eaten chocolate cake sat on a desk at the side of the room. It had been delivered to the class by Renwick's Restaurant, where Mrs. Hsu is head chef. Careful icing script had spelled out THANKS TO MARY ANNE AND HER WONDERFUL CLASS!

Wasn't that nice? A little embarrassing, too. Dawn had been right. Shelley did make a fuss over me in class. She called me "Most Improved Student" and said that everyone should think about me whenever they face an emergency.

It felt great, but, to be honest, I was a bit tired of the attention. Remember when I said that Jeff and Dawn had disappeared into the kitchen during my conversation with Logan the afternoon before? That was because they were laying out a special lunch they'd ordered from my favorite gourmet Chinese restaurant, Uncle Ed's.

Later on, at Monday's BSC meeting, Claudia had taken out a bag full of Skor bars (which I adore) and served Hostess cupcakes decorated with letters of my name spelled out in Alpha-Bits.

The cake from Renwick's, I was sure, would be the end of it.

As Kristy and I left the room, we hugged Shelley, then took small pieces of cake on a napkin (one for me, three for Kristy).

All of us BSC members gathered outside the classroom to reminisce. Before long, Abby and Kristy split off to go home, and the rest of us headed toward my neighborhood.

Logan was hardly speaking. He looked nervous. This was The Big Day. He'd warned his parents that he wanted to discuss "the future" around 5:30, right after Mr. Bruno returned from work — and that I was going to be there.

Mr. Bruno's reaction? "You're not planning on getting married, are you?"

(Talk about embarrassing!)

Surrounded by our friends on the walk home, Logan looked petrified. He didn't speak at all, aside from a quick "Good-bye" in front of his house.

Dawn, of course, knew exactly what was going on. As we walked through our front door, she said, "I'll bet he calls you three times before five o'clock."

Rrrrrinnnng!

We burst into laughter. You know what? It *was* Logan.

And by five o'clock, he had called *four* times.

First he decided he didn't want me to come over. Then he decided he wanted me to do all the talking. Then he wanted to postpone it a day.

Finally we decided to go ahead just the way we'd planned. I walked over to his house at 5:15. Logan was waiting for me at the front door, wearing his football jersey.

"Hi," he said. "Come on in."

Logan's younger brother and sister, Hunter and Kerry, came running in. "Are you really getting married?" Hunter asked.

"Arrrgggghhh!" Logan growled like a tiger.

The kids went squealing through the house and out the back door.

"Some refreshments!" Mrs. Bruno called out, bringing in a platter of crackers, cheese, and juice.

"Thanks," I said.

Logan picked up a slice of Brie and grimaced. "Smells like old sweatsocks."

I glared at him. "Lo-*gan*."

Mrs. Bruno was chuckling. "Try some. It builds character."

Logan kind of choked up then.

At first I thought he'd taken the remark as an insult. Then I saw him looking outside. His face seemed to lose color.

Mr. Bruno's car was pulling up the driveway.

I tried to send Logan a telepathic message: *Be brave.*

A moment later, Mr. Bruno bounded in the front door. "Afternoon, everybody!"

Crash! went the back door.

"Daddyyyyyy!" screamed Hunter and Kerry.

Hugs, kisses, squeals — and out they ran.

Crash! went the back door again.

Chuckling, Mr. Bruno sat on the sofa. His nose began to twitch. "What smells?"

"The cheese, dear," Mrs. Bruno replied dryly.

I don't know how I kept from cracking up.

Poor Logan. He wasn't seeing the humor in any of this. He was biting his fingernails. His forehead was shiny from sweat.

"So, when's the big date, and how much is the cake going to cost?" Mr. Bruno asked with a big laugh.

I could feel myself blushing. Logan was turning red, too.

His mouth opened and quickly shut. He glanced at me, his eyes wide and unsure.

He's not going to do it, I thought.

"What is it, dear?" Mrs. Bruno asked.

Well, if Logan wasn't going to break the ice, I would. I cleared my throat and began, "Logan would like to — "

"Dad, Mom?" Logan blurted out. "I don't want to go to Conant."

Ta-da. Nothing like the whole truth upfront.

"Logan," his dad said sternly. "You know we've discussed this — "

"And I don't want to go to leadership camp, either," Logan barreled on. "I want to play in the summer baseball league and stay in the Stoneybrook public schools, and that's that."

I sat back. He was doing it. He was doing it all by himself.

"Dear, I know you're reluctant to go away," his mother said. "It isn't easy to leave home."

"Conant is a special world," Mr. Bruno said. "I was a lazy, uninterested student before I arrived there. I'd never played a sport in my life. Well, the moment I set foot on that extraordinary campus, my life turned around. The academics, the sports, the activities — it was a whole new experience. I want that for you, too, Logan."

"I have it all already, Dad," Logan said, "in Stoneybrook! I mean, if Stoneybrook were so awful, I could see what you mean, but it's not."

Mr. Bruno looked perplexed. "I'm a little surprised at you, Logan. A lot of boys would be thrilled at this opportunity."

Logan sat back and sighed deeply. "I know what Conant meant to you, Dad. I'm sure it changed your life. But I just don't see how you think it'll change mine. I'm a different kind of person. I mean, I'm not trying to sound conceited, but my grades are already good. And I played three sports this year."

"He has a point, Lyman," Mrs. Bruno said.

"But you'll meet boys from all over the country," Mr. Bruno pressed on. "Interesting, bright, friendly . . ."

"That's cool, but I like *my* friends. Guys *and* girls." Logan gave me a quick look, then glanced back to his father. "Dad, I appreciate what you're trying to do. Really. But you're laying out all this money for stuff I don't need. For stuff I already *have*. I'm happy here. I like Stoneybrook. I like living at home with you guys. I don't want to come here only for visits and see my brother and sister growing up without me. I don't need to leave home."

"Well," Mr. Bruno said with a frown, "you realize I've already put down a deposit. If you'd really felt that strongly about this, you could have mentioned it earlier."

"Oh, honey, it's been clear that Logan is miserable," Mrs. Bruno spoke up, "ever since we told him the news. You've noticed it yourself."

"I'll pay back the deposit," Logan volunteered eagerly, "out of my earnings from the Rosebud. Even if it takes all year."

"*I'll* pay from *my* earnings if I have to," Mrs. Bruno declared. "I like having my son around the house."

Wow. Logan and I both turned to her with big grins.

But her jaw was set solid. And she was glaring at her husband.

Mr. Bruno cleared his throat and picked up a cracker with cheese.

No one said a word as he fiddled with it, then popped it in his mouth. Slowly he chewed, looking vaguely in the direction of the window.

Logan gulped.

I could feel perspiration clamming up my blouse. The silence was killing me.

Finally Mr. Bruno swallowed. He scowled darkly at Logan and said, "Do you think you could bring back a better-tasting hunk of cheese from the Rosebud this summer?"

"I beg your pardon?" Logan's mom said, with a look of mock horror.

Mr. Bruno was trying hard not to crack a smile — but not hard enough.

Logan's jaw dropped open. He was looking at his father as if Mr. Bruno had just sprouted corn behind his ears. "You — you mean — ?"

Mr. Bruno burst out laughing. "You're a Bruno! You make a good argument, son. What can I say?"

Then Logan did something I never dreamed I'd see him do. He leaped at his dad and wrapped his arms around him.

I was almost positive he said, "I love you, Dad." But I couldn't be sure.

The sound of my sniffles blocked out the words.

Or maybe they were Mrs. Bruno's sniffles.

Right then, we kind of sounded the same.

Dear Reader,

In *Mary Anne to the Rescue*, Mary Anne must deal with an unexpected emergency — with an accident. And that's just the thing about accidents, they're unexpected. You never know when one is going to happen, or what is going to happen. When I was a baby-sitter, I dealt with typical emergencies — bee stings, skinned knees, and so forth. Fortunately, I never had to deal with big emergencies, like Mary Anne's. Still, you never know what to expect. There was a time a sitting charge got his hand stuck up the vacuum cleaner. Another charge got his foot caught in the spokes of a moving bike. It was gross, but I had to deal with it. So it's good to be prepared for anything.

Lots of organizations offer first-aid courses and safe sitting courses. You might also want to take a baby and child care class. The important thing (and something that Mary Anne found out) is that the more prepared you are, the more confident you'll be when you're sitting. And a confident baby-sitter is a good baby-sitter.

Happy reading,

Ann M Martin

Ann M. Martin

About the Author

ANN MATTHEWS MARTIN was born on August 12, 1955. She grew up in Princeton, NJ, with her parents and heı younger sister, Jane.

Although Ann used to be a teacher and then an editor of children's books, she's now a full-time writer. She gets the ideas for her books from many different places. Some are based on personal experiences. Others are based on childhood memories and feelings. Many are written about contemporary problems or events.

All of Ann's characters, even the members of the Baby-sitters Club, are made up. (So is Stoneybrook.) But many of her characters are based on real people. Sometimes Ann names her characters after people she knows, other times she chooses names she likes.

In addition to the Baby-sitters Club books, Ann Martin has written many other books for children. Her favorite is *Ten Kids, No Pets* because she loves big families and she loves animals. Her favorite Baby-sitters Club book is *Kristy's Big Day*. (By the way, Kristy is her favorite baby-sitter!)

Ann M. Martin now lives in New York with her cats, Gussie and Woody. Her hobbies are reading, sewing, and needlework — especially making clothes for children.

Notebook Pages

This Baby-sitters Club book belongs to ______________________.

I am ____________ years old and in the ______________________

grade.

The name of my school is ______________________________.

I got this BSC book from ______________________________.

I started reading it on ______________________________

and finished reading it on ______________________________.

The place where I read most of this book is ______________________.

My favorite part was when ______________________________.

If I could change anything in the story, it might be the part when

____.

My favorite character in the Baby-sitters Club is ____________.

The BSC member I am most like is ______________________

because ____.

If I could write a Baby-sitters Club book it would be about ____

____.

#109 Mary Anne to the Rescue

In *Mary Anne to the Rescue*, Mary Anne faces a very real emergency when an accident occurs. The biggest accident I've ever had was: ____

__________. The biggest accident my friend has ever had was ___ ____

______________. Mary Anne is very careful about trying to avoid accidents. For example, she always makes sure her charges wear helmets when they ride their bikes. Some things I'm careful about are ____

__________. Mary Anne is upset when Logan's parents want to send him away to boarding school. She is very sad, because she cares a lot about him and doesn't want him to go. One person I care about is ____

______________________. This is how I'd react if he/she was sent away ____

________________. In the end, Mary Anne helps Logan talk to his parents. This is what I think about Mary Anne and Logan staying together: ____

______________. If I were Mary Anne, I would have__________ ____.

MARY ANNE'S

Party girl -- age 4

Sitting fo.
the Pikes is
always an
adventure.

Sitting for Andrea and
Jenny Prezzioso -- a quiet moment.

SCRAPBOOK

Logan and me.
Summer luv at Sea City.

My family-
Jeff, Dad and Sharon
Dawn and me and Tigger.

Illustrations by Angelo Tillery

Look for #110

ABBY THE BAD SPORT

Benched. For two whole games. In my whole soccer life, I had never had anything like this happen to me.

And all because of Erin.

I was totally mortified. I sat there as Coach Wu's words poured over me, my mind caught on the word "benched."

"Abby! Are you listening to me?" she asked. Her voice was soft, but very serious.

"You can't bench me," cried Erin. "It's not fair."

For once we agreed on something. It wasn't fair. I was even willing to admit that Erin didn't deserve it, either.

But Erin's next words put a lid on my empathy. "Abby started it."

It was such a little kid thing to say that I looked over at Erin in surprise. She was sitting bolt upright on the bench, her hands resting in two fists on her thighs, her eyes fastened on Coach Wu's face. She looked like she was about to cry.

Coach Wu said, "You are both responsible for your behavior today. What I saw was one of the worst examples of unsporting conduct I have ever seen, especially between two players who are on the same team."

"I would've scored," I protested. "If Erin . . ."

Holding up her hand, Coach Wu stopped me. "That's not the point."

Read all the books
about **Mary Anne**
in the Baby-sitters Club series
by Ann M. Martin

#4 *Mary Anne Saves the Day*
Mary Anne is tired of being treated like a baby. It's time to take charge!

#10 *Logan Likes Mary Anne!*
Mary Anne has a crush on a *boy* baby-sitter!

#17 *Mary Anne's Bad Luck Mystery*
Will Mary Anne's bad luck ever go away?

#25 *Mary Anne and the Search for Tigger*
Tigger is missing! Has he been cat-napped?

#30 *Mary Anne and the Great Romance*
Mary Anne's father and Dawn's mother are getting *married!*

#34 *Mary Anne and Too Many Boys*
Will a summer romance come between Mary Anne and Logan?

#41 *Mary Anne vs. Logan*
Mary Anne thought she and Logan would be together forever . . .

#46 *Mary Anne Misses Logan*
But does Logan miss *her*?

#52 *Mary Anne + 2 Many Babies*
Who ever thought taking care of a bunch of babies could be so much trouble?

#60 *Mary Anne's Makeover*
Everyone loves the new Mary Anne — *except* the BSC!

#66 *Maid Mary Anne*
Mary Anne's a baby-sitter — not a housekeeper!

#73 *Mary Anne and Miss Priss*
What will Mary Anne do with a kid who is *too* perfect?

#79 *Mary Anne Breaks the Rules*
Boyfriends and baby-sitting don't always mix.

#86 *Mary Anne and Camp BSC*
Mary Anne is in for loads of summer fun!

#93 *Mary Anne and the Memory Garden*
Mary Anne must say a sad good-bye to a friend.

#102 *Mary Anne and the Little Princess*
Mary Anne is sitting for an heir to the British throne!

#109 *Mary Anne to the Rescue*
Can Mary Anne stand the pressure of a life-or-death emergency?

Mysteries:

#5 *Mary Anne and the Secret in the Attic*
Mary Anne discovers a secret about her past and now she's afraid of the future!

#13 *Mary Anne and the Library Mystery*
There's a readathon going on and someone's setting fires in the Stoneybrook Library!

#20 *Mary Anne and the Zoo Mystery*
Someone is freeing the animals at the Bedford Zoo!

#24 *Mary Anne and the Silent Witness*
Luke knows who did it — but can Mary Anne convince him to tell?

Portrait Collection:

Mary Anne's Book
Mary Anne's own life story.